Mr. MERLIN

Episode 1

Mr. MERLIN

Episode 1

Novelization by **William Rotsler**
based on a teleplay by Larry Tucker
and Larry Rosen

Wanderer Books
Published by Simon & Schuster, New York

Copyright © 1981 by Columbia Pictures Television,
A division of Columbia Pictures
Industries, Inc.
Published by WANDERER BOOKS
A Simon & Schuster Division of
Gulf & Western Corporation
1230 Avenue of the Americas
New York, New York 10020

Designed by Ginger Giles
Manufactured in the United States of America
10 9 8 7 6 5 4 3 2 1

WANDERER and colophon are trademarks
of Simon & Schuster

Library of Congress Cataloging in Publication Data

Rotsler, William.
Mr. Merlin, episode #1.

Summary: Max Merlin, mechanic and magician,
reminisces about Camelot while facing the reality
of breaking in a new apprentice in twentieth-
century San Francisco.
[1. Merlin—Fiction. 2. Magic—Fiction]
I. Tucker, Larry. II. Rosen, Larry. III. Title.
PZ7.R753Mr [Fic] 81-14772
ISBN 0-671-44479-4 AACR2

Chapter One

It was one of those crystal-clear days in San Francisco that made you feel so good you thought anything could happen. And you hoped it would.

There were boats in the bay, swinging out toward Alcatraz Island, and lovers in the parks. The Golden Gate stood gracefully spanning the gap, red-orange and bearing its usual load of cars. Coit Tower, once the highest point in Baghdad-by-the-Bay, was just another building in the new tower city. Along the Embarcadero, artists were selling original oil paintings, jewelry, and pots. Ladies in gypsylike clothing would read your palm and give you a glimpse into the future.

In front of a gas station garage near downtown, a crowbar stood imbedded in a small oil drum filled with cement. Hanging from the black metal bar was a homemade sign indicating HELP WANTED. Nearby, sitting on the curb by the restrooms, was a tall, dark young man with a red bandanna tied around his long hair. His black leather jacket was studded with chrome stars and diamonds. He seemed to be talking to a pair of legs protruding out from under a car with an open hood. The legs wore denim and the shoes were scuffed.

Next to the young man sat his girlfriend, staring off at the skyline and mindlessly blowing bubbles with her gum and popping them with a sharp *tok!*

"Full-time work I don't need," the young man said, "but this could be a great part-time job for me." He checked that the man under the car couldn't see him, picked up a crescent wrench, and dropped it into the girl's purse. "My friends could hang around," he continued, "fix their motor-cycles and stuff." An open-ended, half-inch wrench clinked into the purse.

A wry voice came from under the car. "Sounds wonderful." There was the sound of some hammering, then another loud *pop* of bursting bubble gum. They heard a grunt, then, "Ah ... miss? Could you please stop popping your gum?"

The girl smiled blankly and blew another small bubble.

"'Course, I can't work on Thursdays," the young man said. "My gang meets to discuss ..." His slack mouth pursed into a smile that was closer to an insolent sneer. "Ah ... protection. That's it, protection." His hard, tattooed fist cracked into his other palm with a satisfying noise. "I like those meetings."

"I'll bet," said the owner of the protruding feet.

The young man looked around, wearing a shrewd, narrow-eyed speculative look. "You know, this is becoming a tough neighborhood. Lots of holdups," he said, with a dreamy expression, "fires. . . ."

The little mechanic's cart moved out from under the car and a medium-sized man with thick gray hair and a gray mustache appeared. He wore mechanic's overalls and an annoyed expression. Frowning at the young woman, he repeated his earlier request. "Would you please stop popping that gum?"

She looked at him with a vacant smile and a pink bubble of gum appeared between her lips and started swelling out. Her attention wandered and her pale eyes looked toward the traffic.

"Oh, one more thing," the young man said. "I'd need ten bucks an hour. I've got a lot of expenses," he explained, looking around for an example. "Jane isn't cheap," he added.

Tok!

An expression of annoyance crossed the gray-haired man's face before it resumed its normal, slightly mischievous look. "Must cost you over a hundred dollars a week for gum," he said.

The young man frowned, trying to calculate the true amount, but the older man was already speaking to the bland young woman. "Blow a big bubble," he urged.

"Sure," she said, happy to display her talents.

The pink bubble appeared from her lips and slowly grew to the size of a large apple.

"Bigger!" the mechanic insisted.

The bubble, swollen to the size of a basketball, made the young woman's eyes focus and become wide. Her mouth and cheeks moved as if to pop the bubble, but still it grew to the size of a watermelon.

"Hey, what are you doing?" the young man asked. But the gray-haired man didn't seem to be doing anything, just watching the T-shirted young woman blow the biggest bubble the biker had ever seen.

The bubble grew to the size of an over-stuffed chair, then a sofa.

"Hey, Jane, watch it, huh?" the young man complained.

"Bigger!" the mechanic said in delight.

The bubble became the size of *two* sofas. Jane's feet lifted off the cement. She made sounds, but the biker couldn't figure out what she said. He was proud of her, though. No one had ever made a bubble that big!

Jane continued to rise. The young man blinked, then made a grab at her legs. But she rose too swiftly, her feet kicking and her arms waving.

"Merr-uh-murrr-uggle-urr!" she mumbled.

"What? What did you say?" the young man asked, trotting out on the gas station asphalt to keep her in sight. "Jane! Hey, where you going, eh? Wait a minute, you've got my keys! Hey, drop the keys, will you? Jane? Jane!"

The young man fell over the gasoline pump island and sprawled recklessly on the ground. His hand went up toward Jane, who was rising well above the ornamental tops of the Victorian houses nearby.

"Hey, Jane! Somebody do something! Shoot her down! She's got my keys!"

The biker turned toward the mechanic. "Hey, where's she going?"

The older man shrugged, but a smile came to his lips. "Don't worry. She's got enough ballast in her bag to bring her down." The old man's voice hardened. "And when she lands, I want my tools back."

The biker started to run again. "Hey ... yeah," he said with some fear in his voice. "Jane! Come down!"

The wind from the bay pushed Jane around a turret and toward the Mission District. The young man ran after her, yelling. A panel truck screeched to a halt just inches from the unseeing youth.

"Jane, baby, what did I do? Are you mad at me? Come on back, honey! I won't knock you around any more!" the biker pleaded.

The man in the mechanic's jumper

watched with undisguised happiness as the leather-clad young man stumbled along in the wake of the flying bubble. He sighed and picked up a greasy rag to wipe his hands with. He didn't seem to be the least bit surprised or startled when there was a sparkling flash at his side and a tall, blond young woman appeared.

"A cheap stunt, Max Merlin," she said. "Not worthy of the man who advised William the Conqueror . . . or who dated Marie Antoinette."

The gray-haired man smiled and winked. "It was more than dating," he confided.

The blonde in the white dress made a face, then asked, "Did you find a boy?"

Max Merlin looked weary for a moment. "Alexandra, I haven't eaten and I can't concentrate when I'm starving. How about some sushi?" he asked.

The attractive blonde sighed. "Max, we have no time to go to Japan." She made a face and said, "Besides, I can't stand raw fish."

"Oh?" Max said.

There were streamers of multicolored lights—a sheet of shiny, blue sparkles, golden glares . . .

A Japanese sushi barman was holding up a fresh octopus. Max smiled approvingly and gestured for the man to continue to prepare it. Outside the window, Alexandra could see the gaudy neon of the squarish, indecipherable Japanese characters. The noise of the street penetrated to the coolness of the sushi bar. Alex turned away, unable to look at all the ways raw fish had been prepared.

Max picked up his chopsticks as the young woman said, "These quick trips upset my stomach, Max."

Max smiled and offered his plate to her. "Try the tuna head."

"You're not helping," she said in exasperation. "Did you find someone?"

Max swallowed a small ball of rice surrounded by a strip of raw fish. "No."

"Merlin, you're . . ." Alex looked around, then continued in a lower voice. "Merlin, you're a sorcerer, a magician of the highest order, a bit over-publicized perhaps, but with an excellent reputation. Don't tell me you can't find an apprentice." She set her lips in a hard line and waited for an answer.

Max inspected another bit of raw fish, then tucked it into his mouth. He didn't look at her as he said, "I'm telling you, I can't find one. Pass the wasabi."

She leaned toward him. "Do you want to lose your job? It's going to happen, Max. To both of us! If you're out, I'm out."

Max slammed down his chopsticks and frowned at the blonde. "Sixteen-hundred years, I never needed an apprentice. Why now?"

Alexandra bit her lip. "You're overworked . . . and, well, you're falling behind."

"Overworked, I'll agree to," he said, picking up his chopsticks and selecting another morsel. "They could ease up a little."

Alex shrugged and made a palms-up gesture. "I just bring you the assignments, Max. I don't set policy."

Max frowned at her again. "What if I say no?"

Alex looked distressed for his sake. "You accept mortality and lose all your powers."

Max glared at his plate of fish. "That's a lousy retirement plan."

Alex put her hand on his arm. "Find somebody!" She hesitated, then continued. "You're getting old, Max. You're losing it."

Max's eyes twinkled as he said, "I got us to Yokohama, didn't I?"

"A party trick," Alex remarked.

The twinkle in Max's eye died away. He shoved his plate back and stood up. "I can't eat any more. We're going back. Take your tea."

They reached for their cups.

A veil of blue across a field of exploding stars—a shimmer of red, pillars of white, an implosion of light . . .

Alex set her teacup on the nearest drum of oil. Her voice echoed in the garage's emptiness. "Seventy-two hours. We've got until midnight Friday."

Max put his teacup next to hers and started striding back and forth, from lift rack to tire rack. "Alex, I haven't taught anyone since King Arthur."

She didn't say anything, but watched his anger fade into a reflective mood. "Ah, that was a romantic time," he said. "A man could prove that he was special by pulling a sword out of a stone. There was music in that! Such nice clothes. Ermine, velvet, hand-stitched boots as soft as a baby's cheek, rings . . . oh, the rings I had . . . and the ceremonial robes!"

He opened his eyes and frowned at the workman's clothing that he wore. "Now what do they give me? Cruddy overalls, a greasy garage . . ." He made a noise of exasperation and walked over to the crowbar imbedded in the concrete.

"And what's my sword in the stone?" Merlin exclaimed. He seized the crowbar and, with great effort, lifted the barrel of cement a bit, then let it slam to the ground. "A crowbar in concrete!" he growled in disgust.

"Times change," Alex said, but Max made a growling sound. Her expression hardened. "Then stop whining and find a kid!" she cried out.

Max looked at her with a woeful expression. "There's something about kids I never told you."

"What?" asked Alex.

"I hate 'em," Max snapped.

Alex sighed. She disappeared in a sparkle-flash, leaving behind a faint pop as air rushed in to fill the empty space.

Max Merlin wandered over and leaned against the brick wall of his garage, looking out at the city rising above and the clouds beyond it.

All those years. All those places. All those people. His lips turned up in a faint smile as he remembered all the beautiful women who had passed through his life, perfumed and witty. He remembered the glasses of vintage wine shared with Marie Antoinette and Catherine the Great and the others. Some of them knew who he really was— or guessed—and some did not.

He rather liked those who appreciated him for what he appeared to be at the time—a wandering minstrel, a doctor with his packets of powders and jars of ointment, a brave knight, a likable scoundrel, a haughty prince, a cutpurse, and a thief.

"Ahhh . . ." he sighed. Those were the days. People believed in magic then. And that was one of the things that made magic powerful. Magic no one believes in weakens and dies, no matter how strong it is.

Beautiful young women, women who made him laugh, women who made him feel strong and able to do anything. Women who challenged his mind—like Morgan le Fey— and women who did a bit of everything.

"Ahhh . . ." he sighed again.

Where could he find an apprentice, anyway? No one believed in magic these days.

Yet . . .

Chapter Two

Max Merlin's gaze wandered away from a 1975 Ford with a bad transmission, chugging by on the street. He ceased to see the Victorian gingerbread on the nearby houses, the spots on the concrete, the stop sign, the television antennae.

He no longer saw San Francisco in the late twentieth century, but Camelot in the middle fifth. Golden towers of polished stone. Walls that no one ever breached from the outside. Great oaken gates, strong young guards, rippling banners at the tower tops. The stone floors, the woven tapestries hung to guard against the freezing winter winds, the candelabra with their thick cylinders of white wax. The arched roofs, the crenelated walls, the snorts of sturdy horses in the courtyard.

He could hear, as if yesterday, the courtly conversations of knights, the brisk orders of knights to squires, a pair of cooks quarreling over how to cook an ox. He heard knights courting the ladies, the bragging of men in armor, the clink of metal.

He saw the round table, great and inlaid, the center of the world where the truest and the bravest knights sat. That table had become a legend. A place where all could meet, a place where differences were put aside for the greater good, a place where none sat above or below the salt, a place where all were equal.

Merlin remembered making the table for Arthur, shaping it from oak with great swords of light, working through the long night. It was made sturdy to withstand the onslaught of time and the mailed fists of angry knights. It was able to stand against the magical blows of enemies.

The round table was a thing of beauty— polished and smooth, with the natural grain showing to remind everyone of the humble origins of every living soul. It was inlaid with gold and silver, with jewels and polished stones brought by birds from Tibet and Africa and undiscovered continents at Merlin's command. At each place, the shields and arms of the noble knights were inlaid. King Leodegrance, father of Guinevere, had commissioned it as a gift. A hundred and fifty knights could sit at the great disc. Many had speculated where it was today, but others said it was destroyed when Camelot fell. Merlin smiled, for he was one of the few who knew the secret.

And Arthur, bearded and noble, covering his breaking heart with utmost fairness and skillful diplomacy. Wise and just, he had done something no one had done before.

Never mind that it all would fall apart and die. Everything falls apart and dies in time. Betrayal and skillful lies had been the weapons that had breached the great walls of Camelot. Arthur had been a man, no more. A flawed man who had worked with uncommon effort to be his own ideal. Few ever had. Not even Arthur Pendragon himself, King of the Britons.

Max Merlin smiled. Camelot. It had been the time of greatest power—when no man—and very few wizards—challenged his authority. A time of doing things right, of justice and kindness, of good works and better men.

Today, Camelot was broken stones, fragments of ancient towers, and secret vaults far beneath the ground. The moat filled in, the tree under which he had so often counseled Arthur, cut up and burned.

Merlin went there sometimes. It hurt to go back. But sometimes, he told himself, it was good to return even if there was pain.

They called it something else now, naming it after a petty king who had ruled long after, but it did not matter. Camelot was not a cliff of polished stone, not towers capped by banners rippling in the Cornwall wind. Camelot still lived in the minds of many people.

Hoonnnnk!

Merlin's thoughts snapped back to a street in San Francisco, to a gas station where an angry driver honked at a kid on a skateboard.

"Hey, you—"

"Sorry, mister!" the kid called out. He grinned at Merlin as he shot across the asphalt toward the garage. "Hi, Mister Merlin!"

"Hello, Zac," Max replied, his face break-

ing into a weary smile in spite of his melan-
choly mood.

"Job still open?" Zac asked as he shot up
to the garage.

But before Merlin could answer, disaster
struck. The skateboard wheels ran over an
airhose. Zac tottered precariously on the
rocketing board, veering toward a pyramid
of one-quart oil cans stacked against the
wall.

Zac hit the stack with a clatter that made
Merlin wince and close his eyes. He heard
the tumble of the heavy cans and the yelp of
the boy. He opened his eyes just long
enough to see the flailing arms of the fif-
teen-year-old lad strike the controls of the
hydraulic lift and the pully connector on
the wall.

The Buick on the lift plummeted to the
cement floor, its hood popping open. The car
bounced off the lift platform and crunched
sideways into the tune-up equipment, which
was sent skittering across the floor until it
fell off its rollers. The pully chain unraveled
with a clatter and the Buick's engine came
smashing down into the windshield. A bit of
glass tinkled to the floor.

Zac swallowed noisily. Merlin groaned.

Slowly, the off-balanced car tipped over on its side. The engine ripped loose and slid off and hit one end of a tire tool, which flipped high in the air and landed on the dial of the timing machine. It exploded in a shower of sparks. One spark ignited an oily rag. The burning rag ignited a trickle of oil from one of the ruptured oil cans.

Merlin groaned again.

Zac picked up his skateboard, coughing as a whiff of the burning oil got to him. "Uh . . . sorry about this," he gulped. "I just got this skateboard yesterday . . . still learning." He attempted a nervous laugh, but quickly swallowed as he saw the ferocious look Merlin gave him.

"If the job's gone, don't feel bad, Mister Merlin," the boy shrugged.

Max put out the fire with an extinguisher, then walked over to examine the damage to the Buick. "I need something to lift with," Merlin grumbled.

Zac went into action. Eager to please, he looked around for something and saw the oil barrel of cement with the crowbar in it. He ran over to it and yanked at the crowbar, shouting, "How about this, Mister Merlin?"

The crowbar slid easily from its prison of

cement. At once, the garage was bathed in a shimmering light, which grew at once to a dazzling brilliance. Time seemed to stop.

The crowbar glowed with waves of the shimmering, crystal light radiating from the steel bar in the hands of the youth.

For a long moment, the mood was magical. The only sound seemed to be the distant tinkling of ice crystals and a deep reverberation as if a giant had struck a bronze bell. A strange, ethereal music seemed to come from nowhere.

Then the music died, the light faded, and all was as it had been. Zac stood holding the crowbar, stunned and blinking. His voice trembled as he said, "Uh ... what did I break now?"

"Our destinies," Max said.

Pop!

Alexandra appeared. "You found him," she said. Then she raised a cautious finger. "You have seventy-two hours to sign him."

Max sighed deeply, and he looked at Zac with a weary expression. He nodded, and Alexandra disappeared.

None of this was seen by Zac, who wore a bewildered expresson on his face. The familiar place didn't seem quite the same.

Zac blinked and smiled hopefully at Max, who just glowered.

It was a bright room. Sunlight came in the high Victorian windows and dappled the old carpets. Tall, glass-fronted cabinets held precious antiques. Small, obscure statues sat on carved sideboards. An elaborate chandelier tinkled in the breeze from the Golden Gate.

Max Merlin sat in a high-backed, carved chair staring past two candelabra and a bowl of flowers at Zac Rogers, who was happily finishing up a sumptuous lunch.

Gulps his food, Max grumbled to himself. Passed up the pâté for the hamburger. Doesn't know which fork is for what. The manners of a Welsh pikeman. He watched the boy pour the last drops of milk from a crystal pitcher into his glass.

The boy looked up, his face bright. "Any more milk, Mister Merlin?"

Max's voice was flat and toneless as he answered. "Sorry. I thought a half gallon would be enough."

Zac drank the milk, his eyes on the old

man. He set the glass down and took a good grip on the edge of the carved, oak table. Max saw him take a deep breath before he spoke, his voice quavering slightly.

"I know you hate me," the lad began. "I mean, I smashed up your whole garage, yet . . ." An expression of bewilderment came to his boyish face. "Yet you gave me a job." He eyed Merlin suspiciously and let a single word pop out. "Why?"

Max paused, sighing heavily. Make the commitment, he told himself. But the kid is a loser, he argued with himself. No, there's something there, I know it.

The pause grew long and awkward. Then Max Merlin reached a decision. Everything on one roll, he thought.

"My name is not Max Merlin," he said. "It is Merlin Silvester. Myrddin Wyllt, actually. I was born in Wales in the year 381." Max watched the boy's surprised expression carefully. "My father was an incubus, my mother a Welsh princess," he said quickly.

Merlin inhaled, then let it all out. "I am a magician, a sorcerer. They want me to get an apprentice, and you're it."

Zac blinked. Carefully, he folded and set his napkin on the damask tablecloth. His tall chair squeaked back. He kept an eye on Merlin as he stood up. "Uh . . . thank you very much for lunch. You lay a hand on me, I'm calling the police," he finished quickly.

Merlin opened his mouth to speak, and the boy reached for the telephone, which moved along to the other end of the table. Zac stared at it for a second, then his wide-eyed gaze went back to Merlin, still sitting at the dining table.

"You pulled the crowbar out," Merlin shrugged. "Shows potential."

Zac started to back toward the door, obviously trying to keep his voice calm and to do nothing that would excite the old man. "Uh, okay. I think maybe something snapped up there, 'cause you are a cuckoo bird, Mister Merlin, you surely are." He cleared his throat and said with a squeaking authority, "Now, I'm walking out that door!"

Merlin just smiled as Zac continued to back up until his foot hit something. The boy looked down and froze. Behind him, lying on the oriental carpet, was a huge, live Bengal tiger.

There was a long moment as Zac stared into the large yellow eyes. Then very slowly, his head turned around toward Merlin.

"You want me to stay," the boy said.

"Sit down, Zac," Merlin said in a reasonable voice, his mouth curving in a smile.

"I'm fine," Zac said.

The tiger roared. Zac ran to the chair and sat down quickly.

Max began to talk in a normal, matter-of-fact voice. "Now, you will work in the garage part-time, as agreed. But in addition, you'll spend fourteen hours a week learning to do what I do."

Zac gulped. He was a little afraid to ask. This was the nice old man who tuned cars, fixed transmissions, and filled up your car with premium, regular, or unleaded. "What . . . what do you do?"

"I help people," Max said offhandedly.

"With your tiger?" Zax said, looking around at the striped beast. But it was gone. Not a claw mark or a stray hair in sight.

"Yes," Max said. "I have the power to make things happen." Zac looked back at him, his eyes big, his mouth slightly ajar. "I can see into the future," he added casually. "You'll learn to do all that. You'll even learn what's behind . . ." Max's mouth curved into a wicked smile, ". . . the Crystal Door!"

Max's eyes went toward a Victorian door,

which for a moment disappeared, and Zac stared through to a fantastic sight.

Space.

Stars and nebulae and comets hurtling through the void.

Galaxies spinning in majestic isolation.

And a curving, shining stairway going up to a rectangle of light.

Then it was gone, and the stained and polished oak of the old Victorian door returned.

Zac blinked.

"I'll have to talk it over with my mom," he said, his voice sounding strange.

"No, you won't, snapped Max. He pointed a finger at the boy. "You won't talk to anyone about any of this. Ever." His voice made it clear that unnamed but powerful penalties were attached to any violation. Then his fingers made a gesture of dismissal. "Now, you may leave, but you'll be back."

Zac gulped and squared his shoulders. "I'm not coming back here."

"You'll be back," Max said in a confident voice. He reached out and plucked a large grape from a bowl and ate it.

Zac frowned. "Hey," he said, taking a step

toward Max. "Nobody tells me what to do. I control what happens to me."

Max nodded as if saying he heard but did not believe it. Zac's skateboard glowed for a brief moment.

"Not you," Zac said, pointing, "not anybody! I'm the boss of me!"

Angrily, Zac stomped over to his skateboard, stepping down on one end, flipping it up to seize it in his hands. The youth strode out of the room with the board under his arm. His lower lip was thrust out and his shoulders were hunched, but he didn't say good-bye.

Max's hand waved an abbreviated good-bye. "So long, boss," he said with a faint smile. "Have a good ride."

Chapter Three

Zac threw his sturdy skateboard down into the street, hopped aboard clumsily, teetered awkwardly for a moment, and waved his arms as he began to move. The street was fairly level—as level as San Francisco streets ever get—and he shoved off, glowering, as he headed home.

Imagine the nerve of him, Zac thought. I mean, he's a nice old guy, but zonkers! Round he bend, off the edge, whacko! A *sorcerer!* Eye of newt, wool of bat, and all that stuff!

At the first intersection, Zac let out a yell as the skateboard made a sudden turn to the right. The boy fought to retain his balance, then saw ahead of him the worst thing you can see in San Francisco when you don't have brakes— a very steep street.

Zac tried to lift a foot off to stop the downward plunge, but his foot seemed to be glued to the wood. Yet, a second later, as he had to raise his foot for balance, the foot lifted without trouble.

"Whoa! Wait! No!"

He went over the edge.

The world tilted and raced up at him.

Repair spots in the pavement became take-off points. A manhole became a dangerous obstacle to get around. A pothole was like leaping a canyon.

And still faster he went, the plastic wheels humming.

Merlin! He's doing this, Zac thought with a growing fear. "Mister Merrrrlinn, this is—oh! Oh!" An abandoned board and an old-fashioned milk bottle had to be out-maneuvered.

The parked cars on each side went by as if Zac were standing in the middle of a race-track. He was on for the ride of his life, his board magically controlled, and there was nothing he could do about it!

A woman with a baby walked in front of him, oblivious to the hurtling boy. Zac squatted, hunched up, and passed right under her arms.

A car came at him from a cross-steet, and with only seconds to maneuver, he just managed to swing the rocketing board around the vehicle.

A moving van emerged from a side street, and when the driver saw Zac, he slammed on his brakes with a great hiss of air. Zac shot around the front of the truck, up a garage ramp, and down the sidewalk—straight at an old lady with a white cane. Once again, the desperate swivel of feet and hip shot him around the frail bones and on down the sidewalk.

Clang! Clang! Clang!

A cable car came across right in front of him. There was nothing to do but hit it. Zac braced himself for certain destruction.

Max Merlin shoved the cable car operator's cap up on his gray hair and yanked back on the big iron brake in the center of the car. The shoe, deep in the street, released the cable that was pulling it along, and the cable car came to an almost instant stop, shoving fourteen people up against one another.

Zac opened his eyes to find he was still

racing down the street with the cable car behind him. Nothing seemed able to stop him—not even certain death.

A major intersection was coming up. The light was red. Traffic was streaming across, intent on getting to the bridges and across the bay to Marin, Sausalito, and the Oakland hills.

"Oh, no," Zac said in a small voice and shut his eyes.

Max Merlin adjusted his policeman's hat and raised a white-gloved hand. There was the screech of brakes and the polite words that one driver exchanged with another.

And Zac Rogers shot through the intersection like a rocket.

He wasn't slowing down.

Zac yelled as the skateboard magically made a left-hand turn at the next intersection, but he calmed down as the fairly straight street seemed devoid of traffic. Not bad, Zachary, he thought. You know you'd never have the nerve to go this fast if it wasn't for—oh, no!

Another turn—uphill! And gaining speed!

"Heeellllllllp!"

Another sharp turn and he was airborne. He went over a car—detached from the magically powered board. The row houses tumbled in his sight—sky, street, houses, sky, street—*whump!*

He was on his feet again, on the board, which had evidently gone under a car coming out of nowhere. He contined to race down the hill.

"Oh, no!"

Two men were walking across the street with a sheet of glass as big as a store window. Only one of the men saw the boy coming toward them with undiminished velocity. His eyes bulged as he said, "Eddie!"

Zac threw himself flat on the skateboard just in time as he shot beneath the big sheet of glass. He felt his shirt whack against the bottom edge, and then he passed, flying head first down a street.

"Eddie, you see that?" one of the men said.

"See what?" the other man grunted.

"That kid going down—" the man let go of the glass to point.

Zac heard the crash of glass and looked back. He hardly saw the garbage cans as he went flying through the air, tumbling and spinning. He saw a fence, some blacktop, a redhead, two blondes, several brunettes, and his skateboard as he landed perfectly on it.

"Oh, wow," said the redhead.

"He's good," said one of the blondes.

"Cute, very cute," the brunette said.

But Zac was long past and heading straight for the library wall. All of Zac's life passed before his eyes, and he was disappointed about how short and boring the vision was.

The door opened. Zac didn't remember seeing a door there. Max Merlin closed the door behind him and it blinked back to stone.

Zac continued through the quiet library like a runaway locomotive. Heads turned. Books were dropped. A librarian's eyeglasses fell off. An old man stuck out a cane, but missed tripping the streaking Zac.

The stacks loomed ahad. He was heading right between two cliffs of books, straight at another wall. Maybe the books will cushion the impact, he thought, knowing he was only kidding himself.

Magically, though, he slowed down and stopped. He got off the skateboard, which glowed and crackled, and then turned into his old skateboard again.

Zac stood in front of a wall of books, but all he saw was one book. A red leather book with its title stamped in gold.

The title was *Merlin*.

The paper of the book was brittle and old. The sheets were stiff, and the ink was very black. Zac carried it to a table and sat down to open it. He didn't notice the librarian on her hands and knees looking for her glasses. When she found them and looked around, only industrious heads bent over books could be seen. Even old Mr. Silverberg, who liked to cause trouble with his cane, was reading an old copy of *Reader's Digest*.

One of the students lifted his head after a few moments and checked the librarian. He got up casually and gathered up his books and papers, looking over at Zac Rogers. He was a nice-looking young man, nothing extraordinary, but with a certain antic energy.

The student sauntered over, peeked over Zac's shoulder, who didn't even seem to know he was there, and pulled up a chair. "Hi, Zac."

"Huh?" Zac looked up and around and saw his friend Leo. "Oh, hi."

"That was some entrance, buddy. Who was that masked streaker?" The good-looking, curly-haired Leo grinned conspiratorially.

"Leo," Zac said earnestly, putting his finger in the red leather book as a marker, "I've got to tell you something that you are not going to believe."

"You are skateboard champion of Uruguay," Leo said.

"No, this is serious," Zac replied.

"So's Friday, buddy. Are we all set for the dance?" Leo asked.

Zac's enthusiasm drained out of him. His chin dropped to his chest and he looked at the binding of the book. "I'm not going. Julie's going with Steve." Zac sighed. "He asked her first."

Leo made a face. "I don't want to go without you."

"You're going with Susan," Zac said. "You'll have a great—" He stopped as Leo grabbed his arm. Following Leo's gaze, Zac saw Julie.

She was a beautiful young woman with long, dark hair and a graceful manner. She was sitting nearby at a table, and as he looked she saw him. She waved. He smiled back, weakly, and returned a slight wave. Her answering smile just melted him, and he gazed at her adoringly.

To himself, but with Leo listening, Zac said very softly, "My Juliet, thou art a vision for mine eyes. How couldst thou dump me for another?"

Leo grinned. "Not quite Shakespeare, but I get the picture." He gave a light, playful punch to Zac's arm. But Zac's expression had already changed to one of dismay.

A young man, tall, handsome, wearing a letterman's sweater over a massive chest, was sitting down next to Julie, who stopped looking at Zac and was smiling up at the curly-headed young senior.

"Steve Harrington," Zac said in a flat voice. "Why do they always look like that? His chest weighs more than I do."

Leo made a face, and Zac grumbled again. "Even his name is impressive. Steve Harrington, Private Eye. Steve Harrington, Hero for Hire. Steve Harrington, Steve Harrington. . . ." His voice trailed off as he turned back to his red book.

"Why didn't you ask her sooner?" Leo said.

"I don't know." He clutched the book, and suddenly his face lit up. "Uh," he said.

"Uh, what?" insisted Leo.

"The dance isn't until tomorrow night," Zac said.

"Right. So?" Leo asked.

Without a word, Zac got up and strode toward the exit. The librarian lifted a hand. "Young man, aren't you the one who—"

Zac handed her the *Merlin* book. "Great book," he said. "Super. Great plot. Fantastic characters. But I'll finish it when the paperback comes out."

Holding the book, she watched him go through the doors, carrying his skateboard.

"Paperback?" she said, looking at the title.

Golden Gate Park is a vast, interesting semi-wilderness of trees, hills, lakes, wildlife, gaming courts, temples, museums, a Japanese Garden, and out by the sea, windmills. Zac and Max Merlin walked through the lush grass under the pines.

Zac had been silent for several moments, and Merlin did not rush him. "So, uh . . ." He cleared his throat. "So you're saying only this woman Alexandra and me know who you are?"

"In better English, that's what I'm saying," Max said.

The boy stopped and stared at Max. "*The* Merlin?" The scoffing was obvious in his young voice. "You'd have to be, uh, sixteen-hundred years old!"

Merlin shrugged. "I do thirty push-ups a day and I don't eat fried foods."

Zac shook his head wonderingly and continued to walk. "You and . . . King Arthur?"

"Me and Arthur," agreed Max Merlin.

Zac waved his hands. "Sword in the stone. Lady of the lake. The round table? Camelot? All you?"

"All me," nodded Merlin, smiling softly.

Zac stared at Merlin. "Did you part the Red Sea?"

Max looked at him in slight amazement. "I'm good, but I'm not that good." The old man frowned. "You must have failed history, son. That was thousands of years before my time."

As Zac walked along, he either stared at the grass or jerked around to stare at Merlin. "Wow," he said. "I thought you'd be wearing, you know, a long robe and a pointed hat with stars and crescents and stuff all over it."

Max sighed. "I did once. It used to impress the kings and princesses. You have to dress the part. Would you trust a banker wearing a T-shirt and jeans?"

Zac shook his head, still trying to digest all this new information. Max looked up at the trees. "I did have a red velvet outfit that I liked a lot. It was stitched by twelve virgins in a convent with gold thread that I transmuted myself. A nice spattering of stars right across here," Max said, making a gesture across his chest.

The old man sighed. "I used to have a wand, too. The stem was ironwood, cut and polished by the very same craftsmen who did Tutankhamen's tomb chair. There was a diamond at the tip, pure white, faceted like a rose. It came from King Solomon's mines, and was one of a batch of gifts to the Queen of Sheba. It had the—"

"Merlin," Zac said in wonder, not hearing a word of the old man's reminiscences.

Merlin's mouth clamped shut, and he gave the boy a look of annoyance. Maybe this wasn't such a good idea, he thought to himself. You can't teach someone who won't listen.

Zac was looking off into the distance as a smile spread slowly across his face.

Merlin Silvester, advisor to kings, a living legend himself, a man who knew secrets within secrets, did not like the look on the young man's face.

Chapter Four

Zac turned to the old man shambling through the grass. "You said you help people."

"I can," Merlin said, knowing what was coming next.

Zac stopped, swallowed loudly, and made a desperate plea. "Can you help me get a date with Julie for Friday night?"

"Call her," Merlin said.

"She's already got a date with Steve Harrington. He's this big hunk of a guy, looks like a shirt ad."

"Call her," Merlin said impatiently.

Bork!

A telephone booth appeared. One of the aluminum-frame types, but without any graffiti. Zac stared, then accepted it. It was, after all, a regulation Bell System booth. Grinning, he started toward it.

"And you won't need any change," Merlin called after him, smiling indulgently.

Zac hesitated at the door, then jumped inside and grabbed the receiver. There didn't even seem to be time enough for the phone to ring before he heard Julie's voice.

"Hello, Julie? Uh, it's Zac...." His face brightened and a grin spread across his face. "You're glad I'm calling?" he said in delighted disbelief. "Uh, Steve's what?"

Zac's expression changed to one of make-believe sincerity. "Oh, too bad ... No, I was just going to stay home and read a good book on Friday, maybe something uplifting, *The Once and Future King,* perhaps, and—"

The youth broke off to listen intently. Then his big grin returned. He was playing hard to get as he responded casually to whatever she was saying. "Sure ... sure, why not? See you at eight. 'Bye."

Zac hung up, looking incredulously at the phone. Then he spun around, accidently kicked the door shut with his foot, and almost ran through it anyway in his excitement. He yanked it open again and stumbled out, waving his arms joyously. "She wants to go with me!" he announced.

He trotted over to Merlin, who was waiting in the shade of a tree. "Steve's got a chest cold," he explained. "With that chest, he could be sick for a month!"

Zac strutted around, grinning. He didn't really hear Merlin say, "He'll be up Saturday morning, feeling terrific."

Zac swerved around and grabbed at Merlin's gnarled hand. "Thanks," he said with heartfelt feeling. "You've got yourself an apprentice."

Merlin made a facial gesture as if to say, so what?

Zac was walking around, rubbing his hands together, grinning fiendishly. "Okay," he said, "now let's talk about love potions."

Max snapped right back, "Let's talk about probation!" He looked skyward in helpless frustration and said, "An apprentice for twenty seconds and he wants love potions!" He frowned at the youth. "There are some things you can't rush."

An ache seemed to twist the boy around, and he groaned softly. "You don't know what a hurry I'm in."

In a stern and reasonably patient voice, Max said, "Patience, judgment, responsibility. You've got to learn those first."

Zac spread his hands as he tried to reason with the old man. "I want to learn magic first!" He made an abrupt gesture that took in all the world. "'Cause with magic, I could be anything! I could be famous. I could be handsome."

"How'd you like to be rich?" Merlin said dryly.

Zac blinked at him. Merlin smiled.

Shimmer . . .

Zac was suddenly standing in a conservative, gray-flannel suit, handmade shoes, holding a fistful of thousand-dollar bills. He looked down at himself and the money.

"How'd you like to be wet?" Max asked.

There was a crack of thunder and a shower of rain, drenching Zac and his new gray suit. The thousand-dollar bills wilted. Zac squinted up, clutching the money.

"How'd you like to be a cowboy?" Max asked.

"I'd rather be rich," Zac said, clutching the money tighter.

Ya-hoo!

The money turned into reins and a bucking bronco, kicking up divots of parkland grass. "Hey!" Zac said, but that was all he said for several moments as the horse bucked and jumped around a tree.

"Or maybe as free as a bird," Max said.

Whoosh!

The horse bucked Zac off and he flew through the air, his arms waving. The waving arms seemed to work and he began to get some lift. He started yelling when he saw he was headed into the topmost branches of a venerable oak, but his frantic arm-pumping pulled him above the branches.

"Hey, Mister Merlin, have a heart, I'll—ohhh!"

Zac took a sudden, downward dive as he hit an air pocket, and all his attention was on flapping hard enough to keep from hitting a street light. He zoomed around, banked and came back, dangerously low, turning sideways to make it through the cement drinking fountain and a park bench.

"Help!"

"Or perhaps you'd like to go on some secret, mysterious mission?" Max asked.

"Anything! Get me down!"

Zac landed in the grass, slid ungracefully

across the turf and ended up against a tree trunk. He sighed, closed his eyes, said, "Thank God," and then opened his eyes.

"Urk!" he gasped. "I've gone blind!"

Then he realized that night had apparently fallen in an eyeblink. The park was dark with only a single street light.

A shot rang out. Glass tinkled and the single light was gone. There were distant dots of illumination from lights of buildings far off, but nothing nearby. Zac heard a rustling in the bushes and a metallic click.

Whump!

The distinct sound of a silenced pistol made Zac jump, and the slug hit the tree trunk near his ear. He rolled over and began crawling through the grass. "Mister Merlin!" he whispered fiercely.

Whump! Whump!

Chunks of grass exploded, showering his face with dirt.

"Mister Merlin!"

Whump! Whump! Whump!

The slugs splintered a hardwood slat in a park bench and zinged off the drinking fountain.

Zac huddled in the illusionary safety of the cement drinking fountain and tried to

see in the dark. Against the distant string
of lights on the Oakland Bay Bridge, he saw
three dark, almost indistinguishable shapes
run past. His mouth was dry with fear.
"This is silly," Zac said. "It's not night, it's
daytime. This is just some dumb trick."

Angrily, Zac stood up, grasping the fountain. "Okay, Max, this has gone far
enough!"

Whump! Ba-LAM! Ka-pow!

Three different weapons blazed in the
surrounding darkness. Zac heard a gutteral
voice giving orders. "Igor! Spider! Take him
with knives!"

"Mist-ter Mer-Mer-Merlin?"

Zac closed his eyes, then opened them and
saw a sunny day in the park. Everything
seemed normal again. He held onto the
fountain. Max Merlin still stood under a
tree.

"Mister—" His throat seemed to stick.
Everything behind his teeth was dry. He
swallowed, looking at the smiling old man.
"Mister Merlin, this has gone far enough!"
Zac exclaimed.

"Oh? You haven't even begun to explore
the possibilities of the art! How would
you—"

"No, please!" Zac yelled.

"—like to do something in a really classic manner?"

Chink! Chonk! Rattle!

Armor appeared, piece by piece, on his youthful frame. Each sheet of shaped and etched iron weighed heavily on his body. He looked appealingly toward Max, but the old man was holding a sword in a scabbard.

Merlin pulled the sword from the sheath, weighed it in his hand, then made very powerful thrusts through the air. Smiling with satisfaction, he walked over and handed the sheathed weapon to Zachary Rogers. "Strap this on," he said.

"Mister Merlin, if you'd only—"

A helmet appeared around his head, a bright pot of metal with slits for his eyes and other small holes for breathing. He felt like a canned tomato. "Yeep!" he said.

"No time to chew the fat," Max said and stepped aside. Beyond Max, Zac could see Julie, dressed in a flowing white gown, and fastened with thick chains to the drinking fountain.

"Julie!" Zac cried.

But his exclamation was smothered by

a great snorting sound from something behind him.

Dreading what he might see, Zac turned to look. Coming around from behind a group of trees was a green-scaled dragon with a tail, horns, and sharp teeth. No, they weren't teeth, Zac thought—they're fangs! There was something familiar about the beast, which was ugly and very big.

Then Zac recognized it. Chinatown was just a few blocks away, and it had a distinctly oriental look to it—like one of those gilded statues outside the Chinese Palace.

Only this was twelve feet tall and snorted fire.

Fire? Zac thought. What kind of body chemistry did a creature have that could belch fire? But he didn't have any time to think it out. The scaly monster was waddling toward Julie.

"Mister Merlin?" Zac tried to look around, but the eyeslit of the helmet was too small and narrow. He was unable to focus on anything else but the dragon that was coming right at him.

This is all wrong, Zac thought. I'm in medieval armor and this is a Chinese dragon.

But the dragon didn't seem to know that it was out of place. It just lumbered forward, its glistening eyes suddenly fixing on Julie.

She screamed.

Zac didn't blame her at all. He'd scream, too, but he was afraid he'd deafen himself in the helmet.

He drew his sword.

The dragon ran right over him.

Zac went head over heels, not getting to strike even one blow. The armor impaired his movements, and when he got his bearings back, there was no dragon.

And no Julie.

Only a shattered link of black chain remained.

"Ulp!" Zac said.

"Don't worry," Max said. "They just had a luncheon date."

"Yeah, but who's lunch?" Zac protested. "Mister Merlin, this has gone on too—"

"How'd you like the knight business?" Max said.

The armor fell off in a clatter, and Zac hopped around on one foot while holding the other one. He didn't answer the question.

"You don't want to commit yourself until you've seen everything, huh?" Max said.

"Okay, how'd you like to be into something really solid?"

"I—urk!" Zac cried.

Thunk!

Zachary Rogers was suddenly transformed into a statue. One finger pointed westward toward the Pacific and the other hand clutched a moneybag with a raised dollar sign. Max smiled and read the inscription on the base: ZACHARY ROGERS, HONEST FAN OF SINCERE GREED.

"Murr murr ur uh . . ."

The sound seemed to come from within the delicately carved statue. A pigeon landed on Zac's head. Two more settled on his shoulders. Three more fluttered above in a holding pattern.

"Murr uh murr ah oh . . ."

"How would you like to be a dancer?" Max asked, rather sweetly.

"Mug uh murr ma ta murr . . ."

The statue began to teeter on its base and the strangled sounds from within the granite statue increased. Moments later, it came crashing down on the grass.

The granite shattered, and out fell a dazed Zac Rogers, wearing ballet tights, pink tutu, and a T-shirt. He yelped as invisible hands picked him up, and he found himself dancing on his toes on the statue base.

"Yeep!" Zac said.

"How'd you like someone pretty to dance with?" Max asked.

Blink!

There was a pink tutu around Max's ample waist. He looked disgusted. "Not what I had in mind," he grumbled, and the tutu disappeared.

Julie, graceful and beautiful in a ballet costume, appeared just out of Zac's reach. Her long, dark hair was back in a ponytail, and she was imitating the dying swan without even seeing Max or Zac.

"Better," Max said.

"Julie!" Zac called in surprise. He reached for her and—she was gone. "Hey!"

Bork!

Zac's pink tutu vanished, and his usual clothes were back. Zac turned to look at Merlin, relaxing in a comfortable chair. It was Max Merlin's living room.

"Urk!" Zac said, looking behind him. No trees. A paneled wall with antiques. An oriental carpet under his feet, but the surprise was soon over as Zac's immediate concerns overcame him, and he started pacing the room.

Merlin sighed. Zac didn't learn a thing from this, he thought. He still wants it all. I don't even think he was impressed. It's getting harder and harder to do that these days, too, he thought. The old man remembered how delighted and appreciative Marie Antoinette had been with the trays of fantastic pastries that he had conjured up—cakes and sugar delights in the strangest of shapes.

"... And that thing with Julie!" Zac said loudly, waving his arms and striding back and forth. "I saw her as real as anything.... Then I saw her disappear, poof!"

"More of a bork! actually," Max muttered.

"I mean disappeared. Zap! Gone! That's fantastic!" He whirled around to grab a high-back chair and leaned eagerly toward Max. "Could you teach me all that stuff?"

"I could," Max said softly. "But I won't."

Zac was surprised, and he straightened up. "Why?"

Slowly, Max repeated the set of requirements, "Patience, judgment, responsibility." He pointed a finger at the boy. "You learn a little about those ... and I'll teach you a little about this!"

Skoosh!

A lovely bouquet appeared in Max's hand. He reached out and a cut-crystal vase sailed across from a cabinet into his hand. Max pointed a finger and water bubbled up in the vase. Max stuck the flowers in and arranged them with quick, deft fingers.

Zac swallowed and blinked.

Max smiled. "Or something like this."

From his seat behind first base, Zac stared at the stadium full of people. It was the bottom of the ninth, two men on base, the crowd was going wild. "It's the World Series and ..." Then he looked smug. "I know who won."

"Who *will* win," Max said, handing him a ballpark hotdog, heavy with mustard. "This is the next series."

"Urk!" Zac said and closed his eyes.

He opened his eyes and was sitting in Max Merlin's living room.

"I don't like doing that," Max admitted. It takes all the fun out of it if you know who's going to win."

"Uh ..." Zac took a deep breath and committed himself. "When do I start?"

Max got to his feet with a smile and fished a key from his pocket. As he escorted Zac to the front door, he pressed the key into his hand.

"Be back here at eight o'clock tonight. I'll be out to dinner, but there will be an application form on the living room table. Fill it out," he said. "Completely and truthfully," he added.

"Application?" Zac asked. "I thought I had the job."

"I don't make the rules," Max said, opening the door. "They have the final say."

"Who's they?" Zac asked.

"You'll find out. Just fill the application out, sign it, and go home." Max raised a finger and his eyebrows. "Touch nothing, open nothing, and stay in the living room. Have I made myself crystal clear?"

Zac nodded, "Yes, sir." He seemed subdued, and went out quietly.

Max watched him going down the steps, then he closed the door. And sighed.

Chapter Five

Zac Rogers wandered along the street, trying to make up his mind. There seemed to be two major ways to look at all this, he decided. People sometimes live all their lives and never find out what they really want to do. Or people don't realize that their hobbies—the things they do because they want to (whether it's golf, miniature railroads, or gardening)—are the things they should really be doing.

And here he was with a certain aptitude for the business of magic (according to Merlin, the most famous magician of all time). It was a sure thing, if he just would be an apprentice for a while.

There was no doubt that it fascinated him. It always had. He'd gone to the Disney movies, to the horror films like *The Raven* (where Vincent Price and Boris Karloff have the marvelous duel), *Camelot*, *Excalibur*, and even *Monty Python and the Holy Grail*. He'd read *Prince Valiant* and John Steinbeck's *The Acts of King Arthur and His Noble Knights*, a retelling of the Winchester manuscripts by Thomas Malory and others.

But he had never thought, not even for a second, that there was, today, a real Merlin. And running a garage.

Zac grinned and shook his head. Never, never, never.

There could be great advantages to becoming a sorcerer, he thought. Look how long Merlin had lived— and he was far from dead. Sixteen-hundred years! Look at the changes since then! Most of the changes had been in the last hundred years—a hundred-and-fifty at the most. Everything had been invented or discovered in the last few hundred years, he thought. Well, not everything. But all the exciting things— radio, airplanes, railroads, America, television, typewriters, staple guns, telephones, toothpaste . . .

How odd the world must seem to Merlin, Zac thought. Changes were hardly seen all through his youth, maturity, and into his . . . what? His young old age?

Then suddenly, overnight—pow! Technology explodes! From stagecoaches and sailing ships to computer simulation, video games, rockets to Jupiter and Saturn, skateboards, zippers, Xerox machines, and Coca-Cola.

What will it be like sixteen-hundred years from now, Zac wondered. That would be 3582, more or less. The thirty-sixth century! The idea was so difficult to get straight, he couldn't even imagine it. That was a thousand years past Buck Rogers!

Suddenly, Zac was very eager to see the thirty-sixth century. It wouldn't come all at once, of course. It would come one day at a time, just like all the other years of his life.

Zac stopped abruptly in the street as a thought struck him. *Merlin has a hundred years of living to every one of mine!* The idea was so staggering that Zac stumbled over to a bus stop and sat down. For every hour he had lived, Merlin had lived a hundred hours!

Zac considered the reasons why he shouldn't get involved with Merlin. They were easy.

If Merlin wasn't real, he was a nut.

But the things Zac had seen. . . .

No, he has to be the real thing, Zac thought.

As crazy as it sounded. . . .

As totally freaked as it seemed . . .

Zac believed him.

Merlin. Merlin the Magician. Merlin, buddy to King Arthur.

"Hey, mac. . . ."

Merlin, the magician whose powers were unexcelled in—

"Hey! You!"

Zac looked around. There were three tough-looking young men in black leather jackets. A scared-looking girl was with them. "Me?" Zac asked.

"You. Come over here."

"What do you want?" Zac said, not caring to go into the shadows of the evening with the likes of them.

"I've seen you hanging around old man Merlin's place, right?" the tall one said.

"I know him. Starting tomorrow, I may work there," Zac replied.

"Well, listen, peanut-breath, you stay away from that joint. I've got plans for that place. I'm going to work there, see?" threatened the tall punk.

"I think you'll find the position filled," answered Zac.

"I think you'll find the position filled," one of the other young men said in a falsetto voice and laughed.

"I got the job, is what I mean," Zac said in an unfrightened tone.

"You *had* the job," the tall one said. "*I* had the job sewed up until . . ." He glared at the frightened-looking young woman. "Jane here decided to go for a world's record."

"I don't know what you mean, but I have the job," Zac answered.

"*Look*," the long-haired youth said, "I'm Rocco the Rock, see? *Rocco*." He waited as if he expected a reaction.

"Well?" Zac said. "Glad to meet you, Rocco." He smiled at Jane, whose blank look seemed disturbed, as if she had gone through some staggering experience from which she had not yet recovered.

"You don't know Rocco?" one of the other men asked, incredulous.

"Look, punk," Rocco said. "I don't need the trouble, so we'll do this the easy way, huh? You just don't show up tomorrow and everything's cool, okay?"

Zac hesitated. He could just agree and go away and that would be the end of it. Or agree and show up with some friends. Or disagree and get beaten up—or killed.

"But, Mister Merlin picked me and didn't pick you. It's not my fault," Zac said, trying to keep his voice casual.

"Punk, we are not talking reason here. You are talking to Rocco," one of the young men said.

"Snake, I'll handle this," Rocco said. He stared at Zac with a hard look. "I've got no time for this, punk. I've got to take my woman here to some ex-doctor that says he can get her to talk again, get me?"

Rocco walked over and put his arm around Zac. "I like things to be friendly. There are guys here who like to do things other ways, you dig? Like Snake there. He's mean."

"Yeah, I'm mean," Snake agreed happily.

"He never made the debating team in school, you know? Missed by this much. Real shame. In fact, he missed school by this much!" That seemed to convulse everyone but Jane, who just twitched and looked around at the sky. In the light of a passing car, she saw a bubble gum wrapper on the ground and started crying, softly.

"So you see, I'm the aristocrat, you dig?" Rocco said.

"I . . . understand," replied Zac.

"I like things to be smooth. That's why I need that job. It's a perfect cover. Cars, people coming and going all the time. I'll take the night shift. Just perfect. But guys like Snake don't understand subtle stuff. Subtlety to Snake is drinking Lite beer."

"Yeah, beer," Snake snickered.

"Now you understand, right? You aren't a dummy," Rocco said with a wide, phony grin. "I'll tell the old guy that you got a gig someplace else, okay?"

Zac took a deep breath. "No," he said.

"No what?"

"No deal."

"Oh?" Rocco said, his smile fading. "Oh, a payoff! Oh, sure, man, I understand. Snake, this is a smart one. What do you think, Dorf, should we make a deal with straight-arrow here?"

"Uh," grunted Dorf.

"Listen, listen," Rocco said with a smile. "We understand. It's business, right?" He put his arm tighter around Zac. "We all agree. You should get something for your trouble. Snake, you give him something."

Rocco flung his other arm around Zac as Snake leaped in to send a hard fist straight into Zac's stomach.

"Ooof!" Zac doubled over as the air whooshed from his lungs. He felt as if he were going to faint, die, and roll up in a ball all at once.

"Give him a second payment," Rocco said, grinning.

To Zac's horror, he saw Snake pull back a gloved fist to strike him again. The thought frightened him. Something in there will break! he thought. Maybe something has!

Time seemed to slow down.

There was Snake, in the patchy light, bringing back his fist. And Dorf, grinning thickly, coming in to get his kicks. And Rocco, masterminding the whole thing, grinning at him from inches away. Poor Jane was staring at something on the sidewalk and looking disconnected.

Snake's fist started coming toward him. Zac tried to run, which was silly because Rocco was bigger and had a hold on him. But his frantically thrashing legs did pull Rocco around to get a hard fist on his jaw. Dorf fell over when something sticky on the sidewalk stuck to his foot. And Snake fell when Rocco fell, tangled up in the legs.

Zac pulled himself free, accidently kicking Rocco right in the face. Snake leaped over

Rocco at him, but Rocco was putting his hands to his bloody nose—and caught Snake right in the nostrils.

Zac got up and started running. The sounds of Jane sobbing, Rocco swearing, Snake sniffing blood, and Dorf stuck to the sidewalk faded behind him. He ran until his chest seemed ready to burst. Then he went up to a stranger's porch where he could sit in the shadows and watch back down the street until he caught his breath.

After a moment, he lay back, breathing hard. That wasn't like a fight in the movies at all, he thought. I wasn't very good. Everything that happened was kind of accidental. I know that. Bruce Lee, I'm not. But I got away. I know I'm a klutz. Look at the way I came into Mr. Merlin's place. Or the time I kicked the support out from under the painter at school. Or when I was trying to kiss Julie and loosened the brake on the car with my foot and we almost rolled down Twin Peaks.

Suddenly, Zac heard voices and running footsteps. He was lying down and afraid to move. He just lay motionless, hoping his pounding heart might be mistaken for a cable car running wild.

It was Rocco.

"Rock, I tried," Snake said, holding his head back and dabbing at his nose with a dirty handkerchief.

"You tried, my—" Rocco seemed too angry to continue for a moment.

"There was this stuff on the sidewalk, Rocco," Dorf said. "I was glued. I couldn't help it, man."

"Shut up. The punk took us all out. He must be one of them karate guys," Rocco said.

"I don't want to tangle with no more karate guys," Dorf said. "I've seen them in pictures."

"He was good, really good," Rocco said. "Just like those tricky good guys in the movies who let you take the first shot."

"Yeah, and then he took us out," Snake said through his injured nose.

"Well, I'm no fool," Rocco said. "I still rule the turf, man. Only he gets his turf. Only fair. But I think I'll go try one of those studios where they wear the funny bathrobes."

"They wouldn't let you in the last time you tried," Snake said, looking at his handkerchief suspiciously.

"I'll find something," Rocco said, gingerly feeling his nose. "But until then, he's king of his turf."

They walked up the street out of earshot, and Zac sat up. Jane was looking at him at the bottom of the steps. He could see her eyes glisten in the street light. She smiled at him—at least he thought she smiled at him—and quickly walked on, trying to catch up with Rocco and his gang.

Zac fell back on the boards of the porch. I think I better go and find myself a trade. Something in the magical business, maybe, Zac thought. He sat up. "But first I'll need my faithful companion, Leo."

Chapter Six

"There," Zac said, putting down the pen. "It's finished."

"They sure want to know a lot of funny stuff," Leo said from the other side of the table. "Whether any of your ancestors were burned as witches is a pretty weird question. And why do they want to know if you've ever dreamed about metals or seen anything odd in the sky?"

Zac shrugged. "They must have their reasons."

"Yeah, but who is this *they*?" Leo asked.

"I suppose I'll find out." He pointed at the form again. "Do you think I answered this part right?" He read the question aloud.

"Cheiromancy is (a) the ancient Greek god of people who sneeze; (b) the malefic action of black magic, the point at which hate rises to a crescendo; (c) a form of scrying, or crystal gazing, known to the Assyrians; (d) a Hungarian dance."

Leo shrugged. "Closing your eyes and pointing your finger is as good a method as any, I suppose. I passed my last multiple-choice Spanish test that way."

Zac got up and started wandering around the room, looking into the cabinets. A jade skull was in one, next to a multicolored egg. Further along was a leather-bound volume of *Everything You've Ever Wanted to Know About Phenomenology* between *The Memoirs of Gandalf* and *Dr. Moreau's Magic Diet.*

Touch nothing, open nothing, and stay in the living room, Zac said to himself.

"Lots of strange stuff in here," Leo said, looking at a stuffed owl with a stuffed snake in its claws.

"Why, I wonder?" Zac said. "What's he afraid we'll find?"

"You know, I've known old Max for years, but I never knew he was such a whacko," Leo remarked.

Zac stopped and looked at the door that

he had seen briefly open into space. "And I'm not to go through the Crystal Door."

Leo folded his arms. "Zac, my buddy, I've been listening to you for over an hour. You know something? They are going to put you away."

"Huh?" Zac said, pulling his gaze away from the forbidden door.

"I said Max Merlin is a weirdo, and if you don't forget all this, you are a candidate for the funny farm."

Zac looked indignant. "Okay, okay. You want me to prove it?"

"Yeah," challenged Leo. "You do that, Mister Apprentice. Turn me into a baboon."

Zac laughed. "Give me something hard, you're halfway there already."

"I'm late for dinner," Leo said abruptly, dismissing all of it with a gesture and starting for the door.

"Hold it!" Zac said, accepting the challenge. "We're going in."

"The famous Crystal Door you told me about?" Leo said in mock amazement.

"The Crystal Door," Zac said.

Zac Rogers walked over to the carved Victorian door and opened it. No lock, no key. It just opened.

They both stood completely still, staring in awe. They saw the velvet void of eternal blackness with jewels of stars and suns and distant galaxies. They stepped inside, as if entering the universe, patrolling the fringes of infinity.

Zac was aware of sounds. Rhythmic, yet not really musical. The music of the spheres? he wondered. It was as if he was hearing the heartbeat of the universe. He felt as if he could reach out and touch anything or anyone.

The curving stairway was there, white, shining steps, with a rectangle of brilliant, white light at the top.

Zac turned to the staring Leo. "Close your mouth," he said. Leo closed his mouth, but his eyes were still bulging.

"Swear you won't say anything to anybody?" Zac asked.

Leo blinked, swallowed, and blinked again. He tried to gather himself together and feign some kind of composure. "What, uh, what would I say? That a guy has outer space in his living room? With stairs? All lit up? Yeah, okay, I promise."

Zac started forward, then stopped to exchange a frightened look with Leo. But he couldn't chicken out now; Leo was there. And Leo couldn't back out because Zac was there.

They started up the white, shining stairs. It wasn't far—a few dozen steps—but the galaxies were spinning past, turning slowly, suns living and dying as they walked up. And there was no guardrail, no banister.

"Uh, Zac, I'm really late for dinner."

But Zac was at the top, the brilliant, white light bleaching out the colors of his clothes. It hurt Leo to look at the rectangle of light, and he averted his gaze—to look at the Andromeda galaxy rotating toward him. He trotted up the last few steps and stepped through the bright light. Then they saw all kinds of color, right through the spectrum and out the other side. They heard strange, eerie music, and felt some kind of a presence.

Leo was terrified, but Zac was fascinated.

It was a large room, a kind of hall, all very white and pristine. As they moved into it, they could see how the room branched off. Zac got the feeling there was endless space here. But the room was not empty. Everything seemed to contrast with the snowy whiteness of the walls, floor, and ceiling.

Ancient oak tables were covered with old leather books, pots, and jars. There were racks of stoppered vials, a cluster of beakers, and retorts in which liquids of different colors bubbled, scenting the air with strange fragrances.

A live owl sat on a carved perch, a writhing snake in its claws. Objects that seemed to have no known function or meaning to the boys stood everywhere: a system of bronze rings within rings, a silver cup with a raised design that seemed different each time Zac looked at it, a skull with a golden crown, quite crude in construction, riveted to the yellowing bone, a bowl of eight-pointed stars carved from slivers of green jade, a jar of dry leaves sealed with wax.

Not far away was a great globe of the earth, set in a carved frame, with brass fittings brightly polished by use. Zac could see the outlines of the continents. They looked familiar except that they were closer together and the names were different—Hyboria, Atlantis, Numedia. The globe was yellowed with age and in the dark southern sea was a winged crest. Zac touched the globe, then moved on.

There was so much to see.

A heavy chest with three locks and three seals.

An Egyptian mummy which must have been a replica because the case it was in was so new-looking, inscribed and jeweled.

A black cauldron, quite dry and cold, but charred from fire with tiny glistening bits stuck to the inside.

A shield hung on the wall, the raised design on its face that of a horned beast. Another shield had the head of a red horse on it, and behind it hung a jeweled sword in a worn leather scabbard.

There were things on the floor as well. Rolls of parchment. The foot of something huge—with yellowing, curving claws—had been made into a stand, holding a short sword, a scythe, two stout wooden clubs, an ivory-headed cane, and a black, carved stick with a diamond at the tip.

Scattered about were stools and chairs. On one of the chairs sat a tall, pointed hat with stars and moons on it. It was velvet, and the stars were made of silver thread while the moons were cut from thin wafers of bone.

An open chest held a mixture of lumpy

Grecian coins, Spanish doubloons, shekels from ancient Israel, disks of hammered gold from the Incan empire, and pre-1964 silver American dimes.

A brass bowl nearby held uncut emeralds, a diamond that had once graced the crown of King Ashur-nadir-ahe, the first king of Assyria thirteen centuries before Christ, a button from the overcoat of Winston Churchill, a baseball autographed by the entire winning team of the 1947 World Series, a stone from the beach where Alexander first set foot on the continent of Asia, and fourteen fossil shells from the Gobi desert.

On a tall scribe's table was the biggest book Zac had ever seen with pages over two feet long. It was bound in some kind of reptile skin and bore a single word on the cover, carved and painted in gold leaf: *Merlin*.

Zac started to open it and Leo jumped and yelped. He was staring into a rack of sealed jars and bottles. Some held tattooed beetles or colored powders, but one held a two-headed snake.

Leo looked apologetic. "Sorry. I thought it moved."

Zac turned back to the book and heaved

open the thick cover. The pages were of heavy, crinkly parchment. The words were lettered with a crisp calligraphic pen, with colored capitals at each paragraph. Odd, little illustrations were touched up with red and gold.

Zac realized that he understood the words. He did not yet understand their meanings, but he knew he could read it— even if his eyes told him the lettering was done in a language that he did not know.

Zac blinked and swallowed. "Leo, it's Merlin's book. It's all here." He turned a page, the noise of it crackling in the room. "Look! A whole page of spells!"

The youth leaned closer, his lips moving. "How to put a spell on your mother-in-law."

"Good," Leo said with determination. "We'll come back when we're married." He tugged at Zac's sleeve but the new apprentice ignored him.

"How to make teeth whiter," he read. His fingers went down the line of spells. "How to purge a chort. How to summon the Urisks of the Scot. How to respond to the entreaties of Mab, queen of the faeries."

"Zac, c'mon, huh?" Leo pleaded.

"Wait a minute, this is terrific stuff!" His

finger went down the line again. "Removing body hair. Instructions in the art of reading entrails."

"Ugh," Leo said, looking around. He did a double take on the owl, who was looking at him. Leo noticed the snake was gone. Where was the snake?

"How to attract the attention of a rock," Zac said slowly. "How to cure or cause warts. The proper etiquette for invitations to a saturnalia. How to avoid debtors. How to dry worms."

"Zac!"

"Straw into gold. Hey!" Zac looked very pleased. "Leo, here we *go*! Bring me a broom!"

Leo shrugged and looked around. A broom might be handy with a snake on the loose.

"Come on, come on!" urged Zac, reading the spell. "There's got to be a broom here somewhere. Remember the *Sorceror's Apprentice*?"

Leo stared at him. "Yeah, and I remember what happened."

"Get a broom! Hurry up!"

Leo found a broom leaning against the wall between a monkey skeleton with silver pins holding the bones together and a sword with a lot of nicks in it. "Here's the broom," Leo said, eyeing the owl, who was making noises and flapping its wings.

"Good," Zac said, mouthing the words of the spell.

"Zac," Leo said in exasperation, "do you know what you're doing?"

Very confidently Zac said, "Are you kidding? I'm an apprentice!"

"Right," Leo said, thinking of Mickey Mouse and the helpful brooms hauling water.

"Okay," Zac said to Leo, "hold it out alongside you with the broom part down."

Making a face and eyeing the broom distastefully, Leo held the broom out.

"Good," Zac said, taking his eyes off the book long enough to check.

Zac squinted at the calligraphic instructions. "Now, turn it three times and stand still."

"Zac," protested Leo nervously.

"Shhh! Okay, here we go. . . ." He began to recite from the spell. "Exter. . . Phobus . . . Guenon . . ." Zac hesitated, uncertain if he had spoken the word correctly. Then he plunged on. "De Circulo Physico Quadrato."

Zac gave a quick glance at the broom, holding his finger on the proper line. It still looked like a broom. A feather was caught in the strands. Zac went back to the spell.

"By Geber the Azdite, by Aludel, by the alchemy of Hermetic Abdrogyne—!"

"Zac!"

Zac turned from the book to see the broom enveloped in a golden glow. There was a flash, and Leo yelled as the suddenly heavy broom slipped from his grasp, crashing to the floor.

The glow was gone. What remained was a golden broom. A solid, rounded bar ending in a thick, gleaming cluster of bound golden wires.

"It's gold!" Zac yelled loudly. "We made gold!"

Leo stared at the golden broom. He clutched at Zac's arm, and it took several tries before the words made it all the way up to his lips. "Uh . . . does the book tell you how to make a truck so we can get it out of here?"

"No problem, no problem," Zac said absent-mindedly as he turned back to the book. His eyes gleamed with sheer excitement. He flipped the pages back to the beginning and ran his finger down the table of contents.

"Lotus ... Lucidity ... it's not here!" He checked again and there was nothing he wanted. He chewed at his lip as his fingers ran down the words.

"Lucifer ... Lugnassad ... Lycanthophy ... Magister ... It's got to be here somewhere.... Magnetism ... Magus ... Maleficia ..."

"What are you looking for?" Leo asked, craning his neck.

"Love potions," Zac said absently. "Mandala ... Mandrake ... Mantram ... Metempsychosis ..."

"Try Potions, Love," Leo suggested.

"Huh? Mithra ... Morpheus ... Mu ... Mundus ... what did you say?"

"Try Potions, Love," repeated Leo.

Zac's fingers ran down the page over to the next. "Plethysmograph ... Pneumatology ... Poltergeist ... *Potions!*" He gave Leo a wide grin. "Let's see ... Potions, History of ... Potions, Herbal ... Potions, Nauseating ... gosh ... Potions, Terminal ... Potions, Love ..." He stabbed a finger at the paper and let out a cry of glee.

"Got it!" His finger ran along until he found the page number. "Eighty-three!" he announced.

The parchment pages rustled like an autumn wind and Zac flattened it out with a careful hand. "Potions, Love," he said carefully.

"Wait a minute," Leo said. "Didn't you say Max said no potions?"

"Max isn't here," Zac said, bending over the fine print.

Chapter Seven

Zac's confident act didn't stop Leo from feeling nervous. "We shouldn't do this," he said.

"Very complicated." Zac commented. He looked up and around the room. "We need a transmutational chamber. Do you think that's it?" he asked, pointing at a strange machine.

"I don't know, maybe. Look, I've got a bad feeling, Zac. We really shouldn't do this."

"Go see."

"Huh?"

"Go see if that's the . . ." He looked back and found his place in the incantation. "The, uh, Transmutational Chamber." There's some kind of brass label there, underneath the little window," Zac said.

"Okay, okay," Leo said. He started across the white room and did a double take at a collection of glass spheres sitting in a bronze rack of rings. "Hey, look at this!"

"What is it?" Zac didn't look up from the book.

"I don't know. They're strange things."

"Never mind. Everything in here is strange. Go see about that chamber thing."

Leo squatted down and looked into the slanted rack of spheres. They were seamless, without necks or openings, yet they were filled with dark fluids, which seemed to swirl and bubble all by themselves. One was misted over and another seemed to be furiously boiling.

"Hey, come look at this!" Leo exclaimed.

"Leo! Will you—"

"No, really, come look. They are like little movies," Leo said excitedly.

"Leo, I'm busy! Can't you—"

Leo screamed.

Zac's head snapped up and he looked at his best friend, staring into a strange-looking rack with both hands clapped across his mouth.

"What is it?" Zac asked.

"Urp," Leo said. "Org."

Zac got down from the high stool he had been sitting on and came over to Leo. "Now what is it?"

Leo pointed. Zac ran his eyes over the rack of spheres, seeing slightly-out-of-focus movies going on in several of them. Something caught his eye and his eyes widened.

"Org," Zac said. "Urp."

"What are these things?" Leo asked.

"I don't know. They're like dreams," Zac said. "Like dream sequences in movies when—urp!"

The boys stared at each other. "Did you see that?" they both asked.

"Who is dreaming this stuff?" Leo demanded.

Zac bent closer to the rack. "Look, labels." On the bronze ring holding each of the sealed spheres was a tiny plate with the name etched in old-fashioned, copperplate script.

Together, Zac and Leo read the names of the mayor of San Francisco, the governor of the state, the president of the United States, one Rockefeller, one Kennedy, two other governors, the head of the Senate Finance Committee, someone called Marta, two religious leaders, the current head of Columbia Pictures, and Julie.

"Julie?" exclaimed Zac.

"Why is Julie in with these heavy-weights?" Leo asked.

"And what is she dreaming?" Zac asked.

They bumped heads as they crowded closer to look into her dream. "Yup, it's Julie," Leo said. "No, maybe it's not."

"It's Julie's idea of how she looks," Zac said. "No, it's the way she wants to look!"

They bumped heads again.

"I feel like a bum peeking into her dream like this," Leo said.

"So do I. Absolutely terrible. We shouldn't do this."

Neither of them moved. Apparently, the dream had been going on for a time. It took place in something that looked like a cross between a medieval castle and Caesar's Palace in Las Vegas.

Julie, looking slightly older but more ethereal, wearing a long dress, stood on the balcony of a tower. In the dream, there was a misty, split screen where they could see a long shot of the tower and a knight—impractically clad in full armor—miraculously climbing the bare rock wall, and a close-up of Julie looking pensive. Flowers grew on the wall in the close-up but not the long-shot.

"She needs a script girl," Leo muttered.

"Sshush," Zac said.

The knight was almost to the balcony. The feathered crest of his helmet showed over the stone railing. Julie clasped her hands before her. The knight heaved up into view. They lost the long shot. The tall knight swung over the railing and stood before her, the visor of his helmet closed.

"I knew you'd come," she said in a warm voice.

"Many a brave knight lies near death tonight because he tried to stop me," the knight said.

"That voice—" Leo said.

"I waited," Julie breathed.

The knight reached up to take off his plumed helmet, and Leo said, "I know that voice!"

The helmet lifted off and it was Zac. He seemed slightly different—more handsome and confident.

The real Zac just stared. "That's me," he said. He looked at Leo and poked his arm.

"Shut up and listen," Leo said. "This is just starting to get good."

From beneath his metal breastplate, Sir Zachary took a single, perfect blue rose and raised it to her nose.

"Thank you, Sir Zachary. Surely there must be some gift I can give you in return?" she said.

"Only a great treasure, my lady."

"And what might that be, sir knight?" Julie asked.

"Your smile," Zac answered.

"In repayment for the Blue Rose of Shalimar? For the brave knights who perished? For the life of Kardash, the Black Prince of the sunset land?"

"More than enough payment, princess," Zac said gallantly.

Leo started to say something, but when he looked at Zac, he didn't. He saw Zac's lips move a fraction of a second behind those of Sir Zachary.

The handsome young knight bowed slightly, but said nothing. They heard romantic music playing in the background.

"Not a kiss?" the princess asked softly.

"That would be too daring a request."

"Too daring? For Sir Zachary? Was it not

only a year ago that you bested five knights in single combat to take me to the Halloween Sock Hop?"

"They were out of training," Sir Zachary said apologetically.

"And only four months ago you fought in the Great Arena at Ashcumbar to rescue me from the pirates of Alcatraz?"

"That must have been some dream," Leo muttered.

"Three months ago you saved me from the creature from the Black Lagoon. Two months ago you were nearly killed when your sword was broken by the Martian destructo ray. You did not give up then. You fought on, released me from the dungeon, and—"

"I am not worthy, Princess Julie!"

"You could be worthy enough," she replied.

"I pray thee, release me from this spell of love you have cast over me!" Sir Zachary said.

"Her, too?" Leo said.

"Never, Sir Zachary. On the ruined battlements of the Castle of Blue Stone, did you not say that you would love me forever?" Julie asked.

"I was still dazed by the Siren of Sausalito, princess! The drugged wine—"

"You said it. I heard you!" she exclaimed. "And only last week, when you so nobly and bravely fought back the savage horde of Schwartzenbrutes, did you not swear undying faith?"

"It was the passion of the moment, princess. I had been held captive in the House of Oriental Delights by the witch Cherie Gottlieb who had clouded my mind."

"What did you do, sir knight, what did you do that night?"

"It was unforgivable, I know. I should be flogged," the knight admitted.

"Tell me, Sir Zachary!" Her voice was forceful.

"Please, Princess!"

"Tell!"

"I . . . I kissed you!" Sir Zachary said.

"Hey, hey," Leo said.

"It was the shameful act of a renegade to king and country, princess. I deserve the hangman's noose. At least, extra homework."

"You kissed me," she said accusingly. "You kissed me without asking."

"It was only for a second. I was reaching

for my book and you leaned forward," admitted the knight.

Sir Zachary averted his eyes. Leo leaned forward.

"It was only a moment—"

"I know," Princess Julie said dryly. "Only a darned moment . . ."

Zac cleared his throat. "I think we've seen enough. Let's get back to work."

"You still want to make love potions?" Leo taunted. "Looks to me like you don't need any. Which is what I've been saying." His expression changed to a more anxious one, and he stood up with Zac.

"Look," Zac said, pointing at Julie's sphere. "That is a dream. You know as well as I do that people dream about things they don't have the nerve to do. That was just a bit of fun and games for Julie, that's all. What I'm talking about here is real stuff."

"Real stuff?" Leo said, gesturing around the big room. "You think this is real stuff? I'm beginning to think there was something in the milkshakes we had before we came over here."

"Yeah, well, I don't see a sphere for Susan," Zac said. "Maybe she's dreaming of Steve Harrington."

Leo frowned. "Listen, I know. Women want you to be romantic, but where do you go to learn? Movies?" He made a loud snort. "Those actors practice every move with actresses. And they know what the woman's reaction is going to be, too. Anybody could be cool and confident when you know exactly what the woman is going to say and do."

Leo walked off, wheeled around, and came back. "I don't know what to say to someone like Susan. She's not a sports fan, she doesn't read science fiction like I do, she only likes to go to movies where she can cry."

"It sounds like the two of you were made for each other," Zac said, smiling.

"When I try to kiss her, sometimes she lets me and sometimes she doesn't. It drives me crazy. I don't know what to expect," complained Leo.

"They go to a school to learn that, I think," Zac said.

"No," Leo disagreed. "It's natural. They just know how to keep a guy guessing. They want you to be strong, then complain that you're too macho. They want you to be attentive, then hate you for being soft." Leo grunted and struck a fist into the other palm. He walked over to the machine and squinted at the label on the device. "Transmutational chamber, property of—"

"Never mind that. Let's get the stuff together!" Zac said.

"Uh-huh," Leo said without a lot of energy. He went back toward the center of the room, but paused to look at the rack of spheres again. Some of the dreams he looked at were obviously dreams of power and glory, but some were quite serene, almost childlike. He grinned as he saw a famous blonde movie star enter the dream of a man and peered closely at what was happening.

"Leo! Come on!"

Leo pulled himself away from the private screening and came back into the world of Merlin's Crystal Room. "Listen, Zac, maybe this was a bad idea, after all."

"Let's do the love-potion bit now." Zac said.

"I'm not crazy about it," Leo commented.

"Well, I am," Zac said. "This way we won't feel any of that insecurity stuff. You'll know. She'll know. We'll know."

"It won't be very romantic," Leo said.

"Who cares?" He pointed at the rack of spheres. "Is that what they want? Where am I going to get a castle, much less a suit of armor?" Zac asked.

"I've got a cousin that has a father-in-law that used to be a tinsmith," Leo said helpfully.

"Leo, listen to me. This is our big chance. We don't want to louse it up, do we?"

"Well . . ."

"Good, now see about that machine." Zac walked back, climbed on the stool, and started to study the big book again.

Chapter Eight

Zac concentrated on the spell, checking cross-references and making certain that he understood every detail.

But Leo was pacing. "We shouldn't do this."

"Eh? Is that a 'y' or a 'g'?" Zac asked, pointing.

Leo looked. "I don't know. A 'y,' I guess." He did a few more nervous turns. "Zac. . . ."

"Think of Julie and Susan," Zac said. "How would you like to never again hear the words 'strike out'?"

Leo grinned broadly. "We should do this." He rubbed his hands together. "I'll get everything together. What do we need?"

Zac started reading the formula. "First . . . one bat nose."

"Right!" Leo said. He went over to the table stacked with jars and bottles and began scanning them. "B . . . B . . . bat wings . . . bat breath . . . ah, bat noses." He uncorked the jar, fished out a wrinkled, dark object, and tossed it over to Zac, who caught it deftly and set it on the table. "Next!"

"One feather from a bird of prey," Zac read.

"Like an eagle or falcon or something?" Leo asked.

Zac and the owl eyed each other. "Or an owl," he said.

Leo looked at the owl. The owl swiveled around and glared at him. "Maybe we can get something out of stock," Leo said, temporarily intimidated by the bird's fierce stare. He searched through the jars again. "Teeth, tiger's . . . rope, sacrificial . . . rose, eight-petaled . . . aha! Feathers, assorted. Which are from birds of prey?"

"Uh . . . the biggest ones," Zac decided.

"Okay, got it. Next?"

"One triple-yolked egg," Zac ordered.

Leo looked arond in the jars, picking one up and looking into it. He set it down fast, glaring at it. "It moved!" He went over to some shelves and pawed through more jars, boxes, tubes, vials, stoppered bottles, and leaden pots. He finally found several eggs in a box. He held one of the eggs up to the light. "Aha!" he chortled. "Gotcha! Next!"

The elegant and suave maître d' poured the wine into a crystal glass and took a half-step back to wait for Max Merlin's approval. "A lovely Cabernet, Mister Merlin," the maître d' said in a heavy French accent. "Nineteen-sixty-seven."

The old man picked up the glass, swirled the wine under his nose, and sniffed its bouquet. Max tasted it and nodded with delight. The maître d' brightened in a pleased smile as Max said, "Very nice. *Merci*, Robert."

The maître d' bowed, turned to fill Alexandra's glass, then put more into Max's. He put the wine on the table with a flourish and snapped his fingers at the waiter, who hurried forward. But Max was not yet ready and waved him away with a flick of his fingers.

Alexandra leaned forward and spoke

in a tight, hushed voice. "Merlin, we are in trouble."

"Not anymore," Max said airily. "The kid signed." He took a sip of his wine and smiled serenely.

"That's the trouble," Alex said, her voice rising. She forced it down as she continued. "They won't approve him. It's his attitude. He's selfish."

"He's fifteen," Max said airily, dismissing the problem. "This really is a very nice wine. I remember in Brittany in the seventeeth century, there was this little vineyard—"

"Max!" Alex pulled her chair closer. "They won't take him and there's no time to change him." She looked around and pulled a slip of folded paper from her pocket. "Now, I have a list of kids that I'd like you to—"

"We're going with Zac," Max insisted, holding the wineglass up to the candlelight. "Trust me."

"Trust you? You don't even know where he is!" she exclaimed.

Max smiled and turned his wineglass toward Alexandra. She looked at it, then her attention went to the surface of the wine. The reflections from the candles and the lighting of the restaurant blurred and swirled. She saw an image of the Crystal Room, with Leo and Zac at work.

Frantically, Alex grabbed Max's sleeve. "He's in the Crystal Room! With *Leo*!" She stared again, squinting at the soft image floating on the surface of the dark wine. "What are they doing?"

Max's eyebrows went up, and in a delighted voice he said, "Making a love potion for their dates tomorrow night."

Alex's groan made a number of people look up from their food, wondering if somehow the cuisine of this excellent restaurant had made her sick.

Max smiled. "I remember my first love potion," Max said. "There was this maiden, just down the road from the castle of my master, Blaise of Brittany. Golden hair, eyes that could discomfort a man for days, and graceful as—"

"She had this thing she'd do, this look, with her lower lip kind of stuck out. Oh, I knew she was doing it on purpose, and she knew I knew, but . . ." The old sorcerer sighed.

"Max!"

"Lovely hair. Not unlike yours, my dear. Well, I was just paralyzed—couldn't eat, couldn't get a spell right to save my soul. Twice I confused fragrances and once I even used too much wortleaf. But I finally got it right. It worked half the night after my master had gone into meditation. It made the nicest little love potion you—"

"Max!" Alexandra grabbed the rich fabric of his dinner jacket. "That's just the kind of thing they object to, you know that!"

"I used the older incantation, of course. Troll sweat, some dried leaves from this little flower that used to grow in the cracks of the palace of Sargon." Merlin shook his head wearily.

"Max, look at what he's doing!" Alex said through gritted teeth.

"Not to worry. I made it into a powder, you see—not all that easy with the mouse bones, of course. I hoped to drop it into a glass of her milk. I was very young then, not much more than Zachary. She was an older woman, perhaps eighteen."

"Max! Never mind that! Look, Max, look!" Alex said excitedly.

Max looked into the wineglass. "Ah, he's chewing up those mistletoe leaves! That's not the way, dummy! You slice them thinly, then use the mortar and pestle! Banging them about with the pestle just doesn't work as well. I don't know," the old man sighed. "I just don't know. This younger generation, so impatient!"

"Max, they just won't allow anyone like this to—"

"He'll be ready," Max calmly said.

Alexandra looked skeptical. "You're going to teach him to be a giving, selfless person in twenty-four hours?" She sniffed and sat back, folding her arms. "It can't be done."

Max grinned at her. "Did I teach Attila the Hun to brush his teeth?"

"You did."

"Who was it that told that kid Washington what to say when the dope chopped down the cherry tree?" Max asked.

"You did."

"And who got Caligula to eat with a knife and fork?"

"You did, Max."

"The defense rests," Max concluded smugly. He swirled his glass of wine and the image in it disappeared.

"Is there enough dried Nile grass, do you think?" Leo asked.

"Yes," Zac said. "I do wish we could have found some jellied crocodile liver bits, though."

"The alligator stuff should be just as good, right?" Leo asked.

"Why do you think the spell wants that stuff, anyway? It doesn't sound very loving to me," Zac said. "Do we have everything?"

Leo looked into the beaker with an expression of mixed emotion. "I hope it works better than it smells. Whew!"

"Never mind, let's pour it in," Zac said.

They took the beaker over to a polished brass machine with a slot-machine handle, two funnels on top, a copper-rimmed number indicator, and an opening at the bottom.

"It looks like something from one of those Vincent Price movies set in the last century," Leo muttered.

"Never mind that. We're ready. It's still bubbling. Set it on number two."

Leo turned the indicator until the number "2" showed in the window. Then, with trembling hands, Zac poured the noxious fluid into the top funnels—half in one funnel, half in the other.

Pong! Tink! Gurgle.

Ump, ump, ump, pop!

The number indicator clunked to zero, and a puff of pinkish smoke drifted out of the two top funnels. Two pink tablets fell into the receptacle at the bottom. They glowed briefly and then all was quiet.

"They look like two pink Alka-Seltzers," Leo said.

"And relief is just a swallow away," Zac grinned.

They fished the two pink disks from the receptacle and stared at them with fiendish delight.

"Oh, boy," Leo said.

"My sentiments exactly," Zac said.

"At last," Leo said.

"Oh, yes, at last," Zac said.

The restaurant at the top of the Wellington Hotel had the third-best view of San Francisco in the area. The city seemed to be an arrangement of lights and jewels to Zac as he stared across the dining room through the window.

"Oh, boy," Leo said.

"Shush," Zac said.

"I can't help it." He said "Oh, boy!" in a small, constricted voice, his face flushed.

"Cool it," Zac said, then jumped as a waiter appeared at his elbow.

"More fruit punch?" the waiter asked.

"Yes, please," Zac said. The two youths were silent as the waiter filled the glasses. Zac looked again in the direction of the Ladies' Room. "Julie and Susan aren't going to stay in there all night. They've got to come out some time. Are you ready?"

Leo patted his jacket pocket, then looked surprised as he felt a pulsing of heat and pressure. He opened his jacket and looked inside. A faint, pink glow warmed his face. "Oh, boy," he said. He looked in distress at Zac. "We've got to give this to them soon!"

"Take it easy," Zac said. "We should try and give it to them as soon as possible to be certain it is still working and hasn't fizzed out or anything."

Leo was becoming more and more agitated. "Zac . . . Zac, I can't do it!"

"Why?"

"I never used a love potion before."

"So? Neither have I."

There was panic building in his voice as Leo said, "What if it works?"

"It's supposed to work, dummy."

"I mean, here!"

The young men looked around the room, crowded with elegant and rich men and women, snobby waiters, and the same haughty maître d'hotel who had looked at them as if they were wearing denims and muddy boots.

"Here?" swallowed Zac.

"Here. What if it works here?"

"Oh, boy," Zac said, slumping.

Chapter Nine

Max was alone in his darkened living room with only one lamp and the television set on. On the coffee table was a tray holding several porcelain bowls. There was properly chilled Beluga caviar in one and chopped, hard-boiled eggs in another. There were minced onions and sliced Russian pumpernickel.

From the television set came the raspy voice of the announcer. "It's first and ten for the Rams with the ball deep in Dolphin territory—"

Bork!

Alexandra stood next to the couch. Max gave her a look of disgust. "You can come in, Alex, but you can't talk." He pointed at the television set. "It's thirty-one to thirty-one. We're in sudden death. Have some caviar," he added. "But don't chew loudly."

Alex glanced nervously at the TV set, then at a clock. "Merlin, it's eleven o'clock. Save your pumpernickel. We'll be on the bread line in an hour."

Max waved his hand, which held a small triangle of pumpernickel with a coating of dark, shiny fish eggs. "Not to worry," he said. "Zac is—" He stared suddenly at the set and groaned. "Jeffers is down! That's all we need," he said in disgust. "Get up!" he implored the image on the tube. "Get up!"

Alex stood in front of Max. "You get up and do something! Max, you are being completely irresponsible and I don't intend to sit here and let you ruin not only your life, but mine as well! I'm not going to throw away sixteen-hundred years of good living for some dumb reason." She shook her finger at Max. "Make a move and make it now!"

Max made a move. He reached over and picked up the remote control unit, pointed it at Alex, and pressed the mute button. It didn't stop her tirade. She kept right on yelling—only no sound was coming out and she didn't realize it. Her arms waved and her mouth moved. She made gestures and pointed and held up fingers to enumerate the points she wanted to make.

Max just kept on smiling, shoveling in the caviar and listening to the game.

"It's Galen Tripp. Tripp's got the ball and is going for broke! Look at that man run! There comes Miller—oops! And Tripp's off like a rocket!"

"Way to go," Max Merlin said, closing his mouth around a heaping triangle of the world's best caviar.

Both Zac and Leo had their hands pressed against their jacket pockets, trying to contain the pulsating love potions. "I think mine's ready," Zac said with a weak smile, looking back at the restroom area.

"So's mine," Leo replied, grinning a nervous smile.

"Here they come!" Zac said, turning quickly around. Leo gave a fast, panicked look and saw their heads bobbing along through a partition of artificial plants. "It's now or never!" Zac said.

"Zac, I—"

"I'm going to do it," Zac said tensely. "With or without you!" He made a fast over-the-shoulder check and gasped out his discovery. "They're almost at the table!" He stared at the champagne glasses of fruit punch, and abruptly put his hand over Julie's glass and let the tablet fall into it.

"Me, too," Leo said, getting caught up in the moment. His tablet dropped into Susan's glass just before the two attractive young women got to the table. The fruit punch began to fizz like some odd brand of pink champagne. Both Zac and Leo stared in surprise as the girls arrived.

"Oh!" Susan said, looking at the bubbling liquid. "You guys got champagne?"

Leo licked his lips and restored himself to some semblance of the debonair man that he knew he really was. Proudly, he said, "Certainly."

"How?" Julie asked in amazement. They all were well under the legal age for drinking alcohol.

"I gave the waiter a dollar," Zac said. He lurched forward and grabbed up his glass, hoping they wouldn't notice that neither his nor Leo's was bubbling. "A toast! To ladies ... to beauty ... to love!"

"Down the hatch!" Leo said and drained his glass.

The two girls looked at each other, shrugged, and were about to drink when the pink liquid really started to bubble. Both young women set the glasses down quickly and stared at them.

"What is it doing?" Julie asked.

"I never saw champagne like that," Susan said suspiciously.

"It's imported," Zac said helplessly.

"Hot champagne?" Susan asked.

"It's something new. Jet-set stuff. You know," Leo said. "Drink up."

Leo turned to Zac and whispered, "What's happening?"

Whispering back, Zac said, "I don't know."

The bubbling was so strong now that people from other tables were beginning to notice. Pink foam began to climb up the glass. A woman walked by, glanced at the table, wrinkled her nose, and said to her male companion, "I'm glad we didn't order *that*."

The foam increased, flowing over the rim and down onto the tablecloth. Zac, Julie, Susan, and Leo all pushed back their chairs and watched the mysterious foam grow.

And grow.

And run off the top of the table and onto the carpet, still foaming higher.

A waiter ran over with a cloth and the foam flowed up his tight, black trousers. He ran shrieking into the kitchen.

The maître d'hôtel came over, tasseled menu in hand, using it as a shovel to carve a path. He calmly announced that everything was all right.

Then a lady nearby panicked and started running for the door. Her husband beat her to it, knocking the maître d' into the foam.

The pink stuff seemed to get thicker, stronger, pushing back tables, toppling chairs, flowing over those who fell in the general rush to get out.

The maître d' rose, a column of indignant pink foam, and called out for his corps of waiters, but no one answered. With great dignity, he waded through to the exit, banging his shins only once on the way.

Zac, Julie, Leo, and Susan were against the wall, horrified at what they had wrought. Zac broke from his trance and yelled, "Let's get out of here!"

"Check, please," Leo said.

No one answered. They ran for the exit, hand in hand, plowing through the foam.

"Don't take the elevator!" Zac yelled, tugging at Julie's hand. The others sloshed through the rising tide of pink foam after him as he fought his way to the stairs.

Foam was seeping under the door, and when they opened it to follow other patrons down, they discovered a slow-moving waterfall of foam.

"Eek!" Susan said, looking at the mess. Other patrons, shouting and yelling in panic, were shoving and pushing their way down through the flood.

The foam was waist-high on the steps, but spilled over into the stairwell in great globs. It was light stuff and did not fall swiftly, but it did fall, filling up the space at the bottom quickly.

"Come on," Zac yelled, "before it gets worse!"

They plunged into the goop, feeling for the steps they could not see. "My dress!" Susan yelled.

"It will be stained pink forever!" wailed Julie.

"We'll be stained pink forever!" Leo shouted. "Unless we can get out of here!"

They went down the stairs as quickly as they could, holding tightly to the railing. At a lower floor, a man and a woman came in from the hotel section, wide-eyed and startled. The man wore the bottom half of a pair of pajamas and the woman wore the top.

"Yipe!" the woman said. "Oh, Harry! The world is coming to an end!"

Harry pushed her ahead of him. "Not with a bang or a whimper," he said, "but with a detergent foam!"

A great glob, as big as a bed, broke free from a higher floor and fell down over the couple and buried Zac with them. They fought free in a kind of panic. The woman spit out a mouthful she had acquired because of screaming under the foam.

"Keep moving!" the man insisted.

At the next landing, three large men, wearing business suits and convention badges, shoved their way onto the stairs. "Get out of my way, kid," the first man said, giving Leo a shove.

"Hey! Take it easy!" Leo yelled back.

The man whose badge said, *Hello, I'm Chuck*, shouldered Julie aside and made way for his companions, *Hello, I'm Wally* and *Hello, I'm Jack*. Julie slipped and made a grab for the railing, which was now invisible under the deepening foam. She screamed as Jack elbowed her roughly. Julie lurched forward, bent over the railing, and when Wally ran by and bumped her, she went over the railing.

"Julie!" cried Zac, reaching for her.

The foam bubbled on. Chuck, Jack, and Wally disappeared down the stairwell. Zac waved his hands in the foam, yelling Julie's name.

"Here!" she shouted. "Just below the railing! I'm holding on, but the railing is slippery and—blah! This stuff tastes like . . . like. . . ."

Zac frantically felt around until he found her hand gripping the railing. "Leo! Help me!" Zac seized her wrist, then found the other and grabbed it.

"I'm coming!" Leo said, lurching down the unseen steps. He slipped, falling into the pink mass with a yelp.

"Leo!" Susan cried, bending over to find him. She caught his waving arm but was pulled off balance and down into the pink froth. She screamed. Leo yelled when she fell on him, and Julie cried, "I'm slipping!"

Her wrists were slippery with foam, but Zac braced himself against the pipe railing and tugged. He lifted Julie up until he could grab her waist and lift her over the railing.

She put her arms around his neck in a tight grip. Zac would have enjoyed it, but she was cutting off his wind.

"Urr, ah, gurk!" he exclaimed.

"Oh, Zac! You saved me!"

"Not yet—come on!"

"No, you saved me, like a noble knight!"

Zac blushed. Knowing about Julie's dreams embarrassed him. He'd never look at her dreams again, he promised himself. If a person's dreams weren't private, what was? Why did Merlin have those things, anyway? Did he influence the way people dreamed? Why was Julie's sphere there? His wasn't! Or was it? They hadn't read all the labels, and some were hard to read. But I wasn't dreaming then, was I? he thought. Maybe they only worked when people were asleep.

Leo and Susan rose from the foam, clutching at the railing and at Zac's pinkish dinner jacket. "Are you okay?" Zac asked.

"Julie?" asked Leo, but then he spotted her. He wiped a glob of foam from his face and said, "Let's get out of here!"

They continued down the stairs. "I have never appreciated elevators more in my life!" Susan said, holding up her high-heeled shoes.

They heard the mixed noises of several people yelling at once a floor below. When they trotted down the stairs, they found Chuck, Jack, and Wally fighting.

"You clumsy ox!" Chuck yelled, punching out at Wally.

"You three-footed sack of lard!" Wally yelled back.

"You guys get in each other's way," Jack yelled.

"Shut up!" both Chuck and Wally yelled.

"Hey, guys, let us by," Leo called out.

"Beat it, kid," Chuck snarled, glaring at Wally.

"We're trying to," Zac said. "Just let us by."

"Not until I wipe the floor with this side of beef," Chuck snarled.

"You and what army?" Wally responded.

"Hey, guys—" Zac began.

"Stay out of this, kid," Jack said, giving Chuck a punch.

Chuck staggered, then turned to glare at Zac. "What did you do that for?"

"I didn't, but I should have!" Zac said angrily. "You guys almost got Julie killed!"

"Oh, yeah?" Chuck yelled, leaping at Zac.

Zac cringed back, tripped, and sat down

into the foam. Chuck plunged forward, fell over a step, and sank face first into the foam. Zac fought to get out from under Chuck and inadvertantly dropped him onto the concrete step.

Zac struggled up and saw the startled expressions of Jack and Wally. Nothing moved under the flow of foam. "Golly," Jack said. "Chuck was the heavyweight champ of our golf club."

"Are you one of those karate guys?" Wally asked suspiciously.

"Get your friend up," Zac said, reaching for Julie's hand. They rushed on by as Jack and Wally searched through the pink froth for their unconscious buddy.

"Don't play around with those karate guys," Wally said, shaking his head.

"My hero," Julie said softly as they went down the stairs into the deepening foam.

"Just take a couple of deep breaths," Zac called out to his friends. "We're almost at the bottom and it's over our heads here!"

They linked hands, grinned weakly at each other, took two deep breaths, and then disappeared into the thick foam.

Chapter Ten

"He missed it!" Max snapped angrily, glaring at the television set. "The man's an irresponsible clod!"

"A student of yours?" Alex sighed.

"The Rams used a powerblock on Tripp, but the rookie came through and—"

The channel flipped to the newsroom, where an anchorwoman looked up from a sheet of paper. "This is Maureen Rowland, Channel 2 News. We interrupt this telecast for a special news bulletin. We take you to Ken Garrett, live at the Wellington Hotel."

Again the scene changed. Pink foam was oozing from several windows at the top of the expensive hotel, dripping down the sides, and dropping with faint plogs into the shrubbery. The camera panned down as the announcer spoke.

"A strange and, as yet, unexplained pink foam seems to have invaded the Wellington Hotel in the heart of San Francisco's posh restaurant district."

The cameraman pulled back a bit to show a longer shot of Ken Garrett as he continued talking.

"There has been speculation that this is some rare strain of Legionnaire's Disease. However, it has the color and consistency of some alien source."

Three men limped into view in the background. One had a nosebleed and was trying to shake off the attention of the others.

"There have been only one or two minor injuries," the reporter said. He stepped to the three men and asked them what they thought of the event.

"Terrible, terrible," Wally said. "My friend got beat up by a team of karate killers making their escape."

"Do you think this is some sort of tong war terrorist act?" the reporter asked quickly, knowing a lead when he saw one.

"They jumped me," Chuck said. "We couldn't see a thing and they jumped me, or I'd have shown them!"

They limped off, and the reporter turned back toward the camera. "There you have a comment from an eyewitness, linking this extraordinary event with a possible terrorist attack."

The cameraman evidently caught some off-screen movement and pulled back farther to show a slow, bubbling river of pink foam flowing out of the hotel entrance. It was a yard deep and getting thicker all the time.

"Scientists at Berkeley, however, disagree with these theories and are more inclined to support a more natural cause. Some of the spectators on the scene have their own theories." The newsman stepped toward a police line just as a rising lava flow of the foam covered where he had been standing. He thrust the microphone at the face of a bystander. "What do you think of this?"

"Crazy, man."

The newsman moved down to the next person, who didn't even wait for the question. "We're being invaded! That's ballast from a flying saucer! But think of the significance of it happening here!"

"Here? What do you mean?" the newsman asked.

"You know. Usually it's Los Angeles that gets invaded. Giant ants, things like that. The Martians landed there in *War of the Worlds*, you know. And the first *Invasion of the Body Snatchers* happened down there, too. But now it's San Francisco's turn. We're becoming important, you know. The second time the pods invaded it was here, right around here, in fact."

"Sir, those were motion pictures."

"I saw them on the tube, mister. No, this foam is the signal. It's this city's time to be in the sun."

"Thank you, sir."

"What channel is this going to be on?" the man asked.

"And you, miss, what do you think this is?" the newsman asked a young woman.

"This foam? Some kind of stunt. Hey, look out, fella, that stuff is getting close," she replied.

The newsman turned around and the foam moved up his legs and flowed toward his microphone. "In the meantime, firemen are attempting to clear the Wellington and contain the foam. This is. . . ." The foam covered him completely. ". . . Ken Garrett, Channel 2 News, at the Wellington Hotel."

Max clicked off the television and stared for a moment at the gray screen. "Zac, what a mess!" He looked at Alexandra with a stricken face. "I didn't think it'd be that bad."

Alex sat up straight. "It's Zac? You knew he'd do this?"

Max nodded gloomily. "Yup."

"And you let him?" Alex was indignant.

Max nodded sadly. "Yup."

Alex jumped up and began pacing in long, athletic strides. "I don't understand!" She waved her arms and complained at length. "You have some way of resolving this, I trust." She looked at the clock. "In the next ten minutes?"

Max sank into the couch. "Let's hope Zac does."

There were fire trucks everywhere and more could be heard on the way. Police cars were discharging blue-clad officers who hit the pavement running. There were hoses everywhere as firemen tried to contain the spreading foam, which continued to come out the hotel entrance in a steady, pink flow.

Hotel patrons, pedestrians, and people from nearby buildings filled the street. A police van delivered some barricades that were quickly set up. Foam continued to pour from the upper stories and creep down the building. Some of it broke off in the rising wind and drifted toward the bay in wobbly clumps.

Dinner-jacketed patrons were kept within the police barricades along with their well-dressed companions. Zac led the way to the perimeter with Leo and the two young women following.

"Excuse me," he said to a harassed policeman who was trying to explain to a middle-aged lady that he didn't think this was a demonstration of a new bubble bath. "Excuse me?"

"What is it, kid?" the policeman asked.

"We'd like to get through." Zac said politely.

"Sorry, kid. We're checking everyone. You'll have to wait."

"Wait?" Susan asked. "Wait for what? Look at my dress! I want to go home!"

"Sorry, kids, we have to check everyone

out. There's a team coming from the health department. It won't take long," explained the cop.

Susan turned to Leo and grabbed his lapel. "Look, Leo, I want an answer! What did you guys put in our—"

Leo clapped his hand over her mouth and her eyes got big. She struggled, but he pulled her to him and turned them away from the policeman, who was now trying to explain to a young man in a gray suit that it was not a party in progress.

"Sssshush!" Leo said.

Susan pulled free and angrily put her fists on her hips. "Don't do that!" She looked suspiciously from Leo to Zac. "There's something going on here. All this pink goop." She squinted at their guilty expressions. "You did this, didn't you?"

Zac stepped close to Leo and said through his teeth, "Leo, kill her." Then he smiled at a policeman. He didn't notice both Alex and Max standing nearby, against a fire engine.

Max was wearing standard, heavy-duty fireman's clothes, but Alexandra had her own chic version—a white satin jumpsuit, and a polished, white helmet sitting pertly on her carefully coiled hair. They exchanged

124

looks, then watched as a police car roared up, its siren winding down.

A detective got out, surveyed the hotel from top to bottom with an expression of annoyance, then turned to the police sergeant that walked up. "Find anything?"

The sergeant gestured toward the hotel. "It's wall-to-wall foam in there. A couple of firemen went in with oxygen masks. They say it's solid foam from top to bottom, and it's starting to harden. It crept in under all the doors, through keyholes, down elevator shafts, everything." He shrugged and made a face. "It's going to take years to clean this mess up."

The detective eyed the foam fragments drifting off downwind and at the lack of success the firemen were having keeping it back. The river of foam was now being diverted toward the nearest downhill street—which in San Francisco is in almost any direction—and fire units had been stationed at every intersection to keep the foam moving along toward the bay.

"Any warning beforehand?" the detective asked.

"You mean like a bomb scare?" The sergeant shook his head. "No."

"Suspects?"

The sergeant shook his head again. "Not one. I'm afraid whoever did this job is long gone."

"Some kind of prank, maybe? Those jokers over at Berkeley? Or some of those eggheads down at Stanford?

"Beats me," the sergeant said. "The people that were in the restaurant seem too unnerved to give a straight story. And a lot of them got out of here before we arrived." The officer shrugged and the detective muttered under his breath.

"Do you realize how much of the taxpayers' money is going to go into checking this out to make sure it's not a serious health problem?" he grumbled. "It could end up being a big joke, and we'll have wasted an unbelievable amount of time and money figuring it out." Close behind the detective, Zac lowered his eyes.

Max spoke softly to Alexandra near the fire engine. "Understand now?"

"You're testing Zac!" She looked at her watch. "Four minutes left." She looked anxiously at the huddle of four young people. "What's he going to do now?"

Max looked faintly worried. "This is the part I can't control."

Alex frowned. "You can't control the ending? The most important part?"

"It's all up to him," Max said quietly. "It has to be up to him or none of it means anything."

They watched Zac turn from looking at the pink flood coming from the hotel and speak to Leo. "Take the girls home."

Leo looked at him peculiarly. "What are you going to—"

"Just take them home," Zac interrupted. He looked at Julie, admiring the way she looked, the way she held herself, graceful and beautiful. "You look beautiful, Julie," he said. "I'm sorry I spoiled your evening."

Before she could respond, Zac turned abruptly to the police detective standing nearby, knotting the muscles in his jaws in frustration.

"Sir?"

The detective looked at him with a hard, no-nonsense expression, which almost made Zac stop and back away. But the boy took a deep breath and forged ahead. "Sir, my name is Zachary Rogers. I was fooling around with . . ." He hesitated and glanced past the detective at the flood of foam. ". . . with my chemistry set the other night and, uh, I came up with this weird pink stuff, which . . ."

The detective was frowning at him, focusing his frustration and anger on the youth. "I brought the stuff up to the dining room tonight. I know this is going to sound crazy," he said in a rush, "but I'm responsible for all of this."

The detective blew out his cheeks and the anger died away. From now on it was going to be routine. "Miller," he said, calling over a uniformed cop.

Max smiled. "Now that's not selfish. That's not a boy thinking only of himself. That, Alexandra, is an apprentice. And you have . . ." He took her wrist and looked at her watch. "Exactly three minutes to tell them."

Alex smiled happily and exclaimed, "Merlin, I love you!" She kissed Max on the cheek and ran off to find a quiet place to disappear.

Merlin made a face and yelled after her, "If you ever kiss me again, I'll turn your mouth into an elbow!"

But when Max looked back at Zac talking to the police, he began to smile again.

The policeman interrogating Zac said, "That's a bizarre story, kid. I'll have to take you down to—"

He stopped as the detective grabbed his arm and pointed. "Look!"

The foam was reversing direction, flowing back into the hotel. Bits and pieces borne away by the wind were flying back, burying themselves in the surging pink mass.

The river of foam, which had almost reached the bay, started back up the street toward the hilltop hotel. Under the amazed eyes of the firemen managing hoses, the police, and hundreds of people, the foam changed direction.

Foam came up out of the sewer through the drainage pipes. It came out of hedges and doorways, bubbled up from potholes, and flowed out of cars buried beneath the lavalike mass.

The foam on the walls started going back up into the windows. Spectators could see the pink stuff at the lower windows drop down and disappear. Then the higher windows lost their pink "curtains," and the last of the foam gurgled up the street, through the entrance, across the lobby, up the stairs, up the elevator shafts, leaving the street spotless as if it had been hand-scrubbed.

The fireman in charge called out to one of his men, who was tramping through the foam wearing a respirator, looking for victims. "Delaney, what's going on?"

"Chief . . . I'm up here in the dining room! It's unreal! You won't believe it! A minute ago, all the foam came back in here, right back until . . . well, everything's fine! The foam even put the chairs back on their feet and shoved them into place. There's no trace of foam, not a bit. No damage, anywhere! Everything's in order. People's dinners are on the tables just waiting to be eaten. There are flowers in the vases, a couple of glasses of pink champagne here. It's . . . it's like . . . like magic!"

Chapter Eleven

The firemen began to roll up their hoses, shaking their heads and saying this was a wild town. The spectators began to drift away. A police van pulled up and the officers started loading barricades into it.

Leo said, "I'll go get the car."

Zac looked worried, and Julie started toward him, but Susan took her arm and said something to her. The two girls, in their fancy dresses, followed Leo toward the parking lot.

Zac looked around, feeling helpless. He saw Max. Max smiled at him from under his fireman's helmet, and Zac could not help smiling back. Max was buying a box of popcorn from a vendor.

The detective walked over to Zac and indicated the scene of the disaster. "Okay, kid, do you have any explanation for this?"

Zac swallowed, giving Max a quick look, but the old man was taking off his helmet and seemed otherwise occupied.

"No, sir," Zac said.

"You have a garbage can at home, kid?"

"Uh, yes, sir."

"Stuff your chemistry set in it."

The detective turned and walked into the hotel. Miller, the policeman, came over and got Zac's full name and address and told him he could go.

Zac looked around for Max and found him, once again, dressed in ordinary clothes, happily munching on popcorn. Zac went over to him, reluctant, but ready to accept the certain punishment.

Max let him wait until he finished the last morsel of buttered popcorn. He fastidiously dropped the box in a nearby trash can, then turned to Zac.

The boy gulped, for Max's face was very stern. "I told you not to tell anyone. You told Leo. I told you not to go into the Crystal Room." He made a gesture with his hand.

"Right in! I said no love potion." He gestured at the newly cleaned hotel. You made a love potion!"

Max frowned harder at the chagrined youth. "You're a menace to everyone. You're useless, shiftless—" Max paused as if trying to think of worse words to apply, but Zac beat him to it.

"And out of a job," the boy said. "You're right, Mister Merlin. I blew it and I'm sorry." He seemed genuinely apologetic as he finished. "Thanks for giving me the chance."

Zac turned and walked away, his hands stuffed in his pockets and his head hanging. Max let him take a few steps before he called after him. "You also didn't blame anyone else."

Zac stopped, listening. Max said, "You could have walked away from all of this, but you didn't."

Zac turned around and faced Max. The old sorcerer said, "You were willing to take the blame for all of it." He shrugged. "So, maybe there's something . . ." He held up his hand with his thumb and forefinger almost together. ". . . a glimmer I can work with."

Zac started walking back toward Max, hope brightening his face for the first time. "You mean, I have the job?"

A clock on a nearby church struck midnight.

Max looked over at Alexandra, who was buying herself a box of popcorn. She made an "okay" sign with her thumb and forefinger.

"You have the job," Max said with a wide smile.

"Wow," Zac said, breaking into a grin.

"There's only one piece of unfinished business."

"Name it," Zac said eagerly. "Some kind of quest? Some dragon to slay? A princess to rescue?"

Max shook his head. "No, but no easier than those."

"What is it?" Zac said, puzzled.

"Leo."

Zac stared at him a moment, then groaned.

"Yes," Max said.

It was a bright morning at Fisherman's

Wharf. Tourists were everywhere, but the natives were there as well. Zac and Leo came sailing into the parking area before a fish restaurant on their skateboards, stopped, and tucked the pieces of modern transportation under their arms. They each bought a slice of pizza from a vendor and started walking along. Zac looked several times at the face of his friend before he finally spoke.

"You remember everything I told you about last night, everything you saw, everything we did?" Zac asked.

"Are you kidding?" He pointed at his head with his free hand, scooping in a mouthful of pizza. "In there for life," he said happily. "Boy, I tell you, there's never been anything like it. I'm just waiting for the newspapers to come out. No one is going to believe my story until I show them."

Zac looked sick. There wasn't going to be any newspaper story, but Leo didn't know that. A minor report, perhaps, about a false alarm at the Wellington, but nothing more. Nothing more could be proven, and people would soon forget the pink flood.

"Boy, that was something, wasn't it?" Leo said, grinning fiendishly. "A whole hotel filled with the stuff! Every cop and fireman in sight! Wow!" He looked at Zac with new respect. "Man, I knew you could tell a story, but how in the world did you talk your way out of that one!

Without waiting for Zac to respond, he stuffed another bite of pizza in his mouth and kept on talking. "Furm evvawhar! Runnin' dune da wahls, ouuta dur—woow!" He swallowed. "Something to see, buddy. But what I don't understand is, why did it go back? Did it, you know, shrink or dry up or something? That's pretty mysterious stuff. Maybe we ought to go back and take another look at Max's book, huh?"

He polished off the last of the pizza and licked at his fingers. "Maybe we could collect a few appropriate spells and stuff and run on down to Malibu, huh? We could collar a few dozen beach bunnies and . . . say, you haven't eaten your pizza."

"I don't feel hungry," Zac said.

"Mind?" Leo took the slice and chomped half of it in one bite. "Wug, mon, bech bhunnies, ohl guld and skun . . ." He rolled his eyes mischievously and swallowed. "There are these beautiful girls down there now, practically a perfect preview, ol' buddy."

Zac wasn't hearing what Leo was saying. He was watching his mouth move, the words pouring out, the destruction of everything happening. With Leo knowing what he knew, there was no way either he or Mr. Merlin could continue without a lot of trouble.

Zac could just see it. If people believed it—and that was the important factor—there would be newspapermen camping on Max's doorstep, mobile video vans chugging up to the gas station, people following them everywhere. They'd have no privacy, no fun, no anything. They wouldn't be able to go out to a movie, attend a dance or a concert, or go to a restaurant without a pack of people on their tails.

People would want to be cured of their diseases, get rid of their mothers-in-law or their spouses, become successful overnight, eliminate enemies, or lose a few inches off their waistlines.

There would be horrible possibilities too. Terrorists might kidnap Mr. Merlin or himself, and hold them for ransom.

Zac gulped as he realized other more dangerous situations if this were to get out. If the Mafia could capture Merlin and hold him prisoner in some way—and that might be difficult, Zac thought—they might control the country.

There might be people who would try to assassinate Merlin and him.

Still, he thought, there were some good possibilities—the love of a starlet, the passionate attention of the latest romantic star, the famous Lost Dutchman Mine, or sacks of gold. Or the race results for the entire winter season at Hollywood Park. Or the next number up at the tables in Vegas. Or the Holy Grail. Or a featured part in a new movie.

Then, again, there would be people who would want to combat what they thought was evil. There would be neo-Nazis and Flat Earthers, power-mad politicians and ambitious generals. Everyone with a grudge to settle, a vendetta to start, or a cause to promote would be buying tickets to San Francisco.

Suddenly he knew why superheroes in the comics wore masks. It was not to be dramatic or mysterious. They used their alter egos as protection, a disguise to be normal, without the media inspecting every second of their lives.

Fame would be nice, he thought, but fame you could keep at a distance. It would be nice to have enough fame to make life interesting, he thought, but not so much as to make you a prisoner in your own home.

Zac gulped and said what Max had told him to say to Leo. "Nimbi ... Callisto ... Zogo ... Nimbi ..." He looked at Leo, who looked back in confusion.

"Huh?" Leo said eloquently.

"What happened in the restaurant last night?" Zac questioned.

"Are you losing your memory? That love potion gag of yours almost got us arrested. We were nearly—"

He stopped as Zac waved his fingers at him and spoke again, using his deepest voice. "Callisto ... Zogo ... Nimbo. What happened at the restaurant?"

Leo made a face and responded with irritation. "I just told you! We put this potion stuff in the drinks, the foam started pouring out ..."

Zac looked frustrated and started looking through his pockets for a scrap of parchment as Leo continued.

"All over the street, firemen, cops everywhere. They were going to hold everyone, take our blood or something to test for some weird disease. We almost got arrested when you blabbed and—"

Zac started reading carefully from the paper he found in his pocket. "Callisto ... Zogo ... Nimbus!" He seemed delighted to get the word right.

Leo stopped in mid-sentence. He seemed frozen for a long moment. The various noisy activities of Fisherman's Wharf went on around them. Tourists bought tiny replicas of the Golden Gate, Coit Tower, and the Transamerica Building. Pier One sold some brass dishes. Alioto's served nineteen fish dinners. A kid at the Maritime Museum touched one of the models and broke off a tiny bit of railing. Two people on a cable car fell in love. A man in the Ted E. Bear store at Pier 39 bought $308 worth of teddy bears. A person named Len purchased a T-shirt with the caption Left is Right at the Left-Handed Store. Ninety-seven photographs were taken of the old sailing vessel. A boatload of tourists left the docks, heading for Alcatraz.

And Leo stuffed the rest of Zac's slice of pizza into his mouth.

"What happened at the restaurant last night?" Zac asked carefully.

"What restaurant?" Leo asked.

"What's behind the Crystal Door?"

Leo swallowed. "The crystal what?"

"Who's Max Merlin?"

"He owns a garage." The youth peered at Zac closely. "Zac, are you all right?"

Zac smiled happily and slapped his friend on the shoulder. He felt as if a granite block had been lifted from his shoulders. "I'm fine," he said.

Leo nodded dubiously, then his face cleared and he wiped his hands. "Hey, thanks for the pizza." He gave his friend a pitying look. "Get some rest, huh, Zac?"

"Right," Zac said, smiling.

"Well, okay. I'm off," Leo said. He dropped his skateboard deftly to the cement and stepped aboard, turning it this way and that for a moment. "Well, I'm off," he said again. "So long."

Leo shoved off on the cement and sailed away expertly, dodging a lady and ducking under a kid with a silver pillow-balloon on a string. In moments he was lost in the crowd.

Zac put down his skateboard and tested the rollers with one foot. He looked up as Max Merlin sailed calmly up to him, standing on a skateboard, a piece of pizza in his hand.

Max grinned at Zac, finished the pizza, and shot down the walk, zig-zagging around saplings, a cement post, a trash bin, and nine pedestrians. His impressive moves did not seem to catch anyone's eye except Zac's.

The sorcerer sailed serenely back to where Zac stood, did a turn, and flipped the board up to catch it. Zac picked up his board, and they started walking along.

"You should have ordered the pepperoni," Max said. "It's delicious."

"When did you start riding skateboards?" Zac asked.

"Today," Max said. "How'd I look?" He seemed eager for a good opinion.

"Terrific," Zac said in honest wonder. The old man looked pleased.

Max looked at Zac's tousled hair. "Where's your helmet? I told you never to ride without one."

"You know," Zac said, "it was right there on my dresser this morning, but I was running late and I just ran out without—"

Thump!

A bright red crash helmet landed on Zac's head. He automatically ducked, then stood up, smiling in a shameful manner.

Max said, "Don't forget again, unless

you'd like to wear it permanently." He glared at Zac in a half-serious way.

"I won't," Zac said quickly. He looked around, then said, "Hey, Julie called. She wants to go out with me again."

"And no love potion," Max said dryly. "Amazing."

"Is this going to be a lecture about how people have to like you for yourself?" Zac asked with some mockery. "That you have to take responsibility for who you are and what you do?"

"Yes," Max said.

"Thanks, I already learned it."

They put their skateboards down, and started skating down the sidewalk at a respectable rate—one that would not bring the hearts of pedestrians into their mouths.

"I have to ask you something, Mister Merlin," Zac said. "You know, when I was in the Crystal Room, I saw this big pointy hat with those glow-in-the-dark stars all over it. Do you wear that hat?"

"Sometimes," Max admitted.

"Will you make me a promise?" Zac asked. They parted to avoid hitting a man reading a magazine.

"What?" Max asked.

"That you'll never make me wear that stupid-looking thing."

Max smiled wisely and said, "Trust me."

Farther down the street, Max came to a stop. Zac reversed and came back to him, a questioning look on his face. The old man picked up his board and turned it over, rolling the wheels with his hand.

"Zac, check these wheels. I'm having a devil of a time doing crossover figure eights."

Across the street, a tourist looked at Max and Zac, nudged his wife, and pointed at the big blue-velvet pointed hat that set rakishly on Zac's head.

"Who do you think that kid's dressed up as?" the man asked his wife.

The woman eyed Zac curiously. "He probably works at the House of Magic just down the street."

"Want to take a walk over there?" he asked.

"Nope," she replied. "I don't believe in magic."

"Neither do I," he agreed firmly.